Mixed with Ginger

by

Loretta C. Rogers
Pam Binder
Laura Strickland

Mixed with Ginger

The Wild Rose Press, Inc.
PO Box 708
Adams Basin, NY 14410-0708
Visit us at www.thewildrosepress.com

Publishing History
First Edition, 2022
Trade Paperback ISBN 978-1-5092-4499-7

Published in the United States of America

A Little Kringle Magic

by

Loretta C. Rogers

Christmas Cookies

A collection of stories centered around Christmas cookies.

A Little Kringle Magic by Loretta C. Rogers

Gingerbread Knight by Pam Binder

Snowdrop Cookie Wishes by Laura Strickland

**Also Available from Loretta C. Rogers
and The Wild Rose Press**

Contemporary Romance
Forbidden Son
Christmas at Hope Ranch

Historical Romance
Bannon's Brides
The Witching Moon
Lady Adel's Captain
Cloud Woman's Spirit
Taming the Lyon
When Comes Forever
Bitter Autumn
A Little Kringle Magic (novella)
Isabelle and the Outlaw (novella)
McKenna's Woman (novella)
Fate Comes Softly (Anthology)

Mystery and Suspense
Murder in the Mist
Shadowed Reunion
Fatal Passion
The Bone Yard

Audio Books
Isabelle and the Outlaw
McKenna's Woman
Taming the Lyon
Murder in the Mist
Shadowed Reunion

Chapter One

Landry, Wyoming
December 1880

Doctor Beata "Bea" Inseldorf stood back to admire the small, festive Yule tree. Of all the holidays, Christmas was her favorite, but this was the first year since her mother's death that Bea had been totally alone at Christmas, and she was finding it hard to keep her spirits up. She was also finding it difficult to accept the fact that she seemed doomed to die an old maid. Not that twenty-eight felt old, but in Landry, Wyoming, she might as well be sixty, and as the only doctor for fifty miles, eligible bachelors generally considered her overly educated, too tall, and independent, all of which seemingly made her unsuitable to take as a wife.

Since her mother's passing, Bea had found her childhood home too large and lonely. She'd shuttered it and decided to live in a small but comfortable apartment above her office. She was a member of the ladies' church auxiliary and sang in the church choir. For all practical purposes, with the modest income from her few paying patients she supposed she had no reason to feel discontent.

A chill permeated the quarters of her medical office that consisted of an adequate waiting area for patients, a small room for her office, and the examination room that doubled as a surgery. She lifted two small logs from the wood bin and used a fire poker to slide the cast-iron top aside. Once the wood was inside the potbellied stove, she slid the top back in place and walked to the window to peer out.

Snow swirled in gusts. Only two days before Christmas, and despite the winter chill that cut through the air and the dark-gray clouds hovering above the town, plenty of townsfolk were out and about, completing their errands and preparations for the holiday. Shamus Murphy from the mercantile stood high on a ladder hanging fresh fir garland decorated with red bows to adorn his store sign. His sixteen-year-old son Ian steadied the ladder. In Bea's estimation it should be the lad standing six feet off the ground instead of his fifty-year-old father.

A couple of older ladies bustled past with baskets of goodies swinging from their arms. She heaved a sigh when Caleb and Mercy Johnson walked out of the general store. Caleb assisted his young wife into the waiting wagon. Mercy held their little bundle of joy close to her breast. Six weeks ago Bea had helped deliver Caleb Junior. Bea pushed the loneliness aside. She had many wonderful friends, so what if she wasn't going to have a husband and children? She shouldn't complain when she was much more fortunate than many others.

She wasn't complaining. It was just that the emptiness inside her seemed to grow a little deeper each day, and she was finding it difficult to greet friends and patients with a happy smile when on the inside she was slowly drying up.

Bea glanced at the clock again. She gathered the shawl around her shoulders and opened the door. A brisk wind greeted her as she looked up and down the street. She had no idea who or what she was looking for. Stepping back into the warmth of her office, she slipped into her coat and tied a shawl around her head. She grabbed her shopping bag, then hung the sign on the door that read, "In case of emergency I am at the mercantile."

Putting her head down, she braced against the wind and trotted across the street and into the general store. "Evening, Bea," Olive Murphy greeted her. "I guess it's too cold for patients, huh?"

Bea rubbed her hands together. "I suppose." She loosened the shawl and settled a smile on her face. "Did my special ingredients arrive?"

"Yes, indeed, they did. Your Krispy Kringles are always a big hit with the children. In fact, Reva Stollard swears there's magic in your cookies."

Bea's smile owed more to her sense of forlornness than to gratification from the compliment. "I assure you it was modern medicine that cured her son of the croup, not my cookies."

"Well, nonetheless, here's your order." Olive Murphy, the storekeeper's wife and Bea's best friend, and who also assisted with nursing duties when needed, loaded the packages into Bea's brown leather satchel.

After a few minutes of chit-chat, Bea slung the leather bag over her shoulder and raced across the street to the warmth of her office. She put the bag on a table and set about stoking the fire, then filling the kettle to boil for a cup of hot tea. A howling wind whipped around the building. The eerie wailing sent shivers through Bea. She silently prayed no one would need her services on a night that promised to dump several feet of snow on the ground.

Thoughts of her childhood in Germany filled her mind, reminding her how sad she had been to leave her birthplace. She wondered if she would have become a doctor had she remained in the "old country," as her father and uncle used to refer to their homeland. A slamming door and the loud cries from a child interrupted her doldrums. "Help! I need a doctor!"

Bea hurried from her office. "I'm coming."

She wasn't sure if the child—huddled in a heavy coat and cap, earflaps folded down, and peering at her over a blue scarf—was a boy or a girl. The child's voice was muffled. "Are you the doctor?"

"Yes. Everyone calls me Dr. Bea. Are you hurt?"

"Please, you gotta come. My daddy is sick. I can't wake him up, and he's too heavy for me to get him into the wagon. I come on my pony fast as I could."

A wintry blast from the opened door whipped around Bea's skirts. She shut the door. Then, kneeling, she reached to unwrap the muffler from the child's face. "Who are you?"

Bea's knees went weak. A little girl no more than eight stood shivering. Her enormous, fear-widened blue eyes stared out from the most angelic face Bea had ever seen. She didn't know this child. The odd emotion clutching at Bea's heart stymied her. If she'd ever imagined what her own daughter might look like, it would be this little girl. "Come, stand by the stove, and warm yourself while I get my medical bag." She offered a reassuring smile. "You didn't tell me your name."

"Holly Reed. My daddy is Tate Reed. We live on the Rockin' J Ranch." She spoke through chattering teeth. "We gotta hurry."

Bea placed several vials of medicine inside her

4

medical satchel. "Do you know what made your daddy sick?"

"No, ma'am. He was coughing somethin' fierce, and he has a fever. Can we please hurry?" The little girl squeezed her eyes against the leaking tears.

Bea said, "Give me a moment to gather some things." She raced up the stairs to her apartment. With the threat of a snowstorm, she decided to pack a nightgown and a fresh change of clothes in case she got snowed in.

She hastened to where she'd left the little girl and stuffed her belongings inside the tote bag. When she clasped the child's hand and opened the door, she found Olive Murphy coming toward her with a package in her hand. "I forgot to give you this. Land's sakes, who have we here?"

"Holly Reed. Her father is sick and can't travel. The child rode her pony in this wicked weather to get me."

"Oh, yes, you're Tate Reed's daughter. You're new to Landry, isn't that right?"

"Yes, ma'am."

"Don't you worry. Doctor Bea will do all she can to make your daddy well again." Olive cut Bea a mischievous smile.

"What?" Bea asked.

"Oh, my dear friend, Santa might bring you the best Christmas gift ever." Olive cleared her throat, glanced down at the little girl clutching Bea's hand, then back up at Bea. She waggled her eyebrows, winked, and made a swooning motion with her hand to her forehead while she mouthed *Tate Reed*.

Bea blustered, "Olive Murphy, why, if I didn't know better…" She leaned forward and whispered, "Shame on you for even suggesting... I mean... Oh, I don't know what I mean."

"I do believe you're blushing."

"I am not. My cheeks are red from the cold. Anyhow, all your nonsense aside, I was just coming to let you know that, depending on the snowy conditions, I may be gone for several days. Would you mind terribly filling in while I'm away?"

"Barring no dire emergencies like a ruptured appendix, you know I'll do what I can." Olive called over her shoulder to the young man propped against a pickle barrel. "Ian, take your lazy self to the livery and tell Mr. Hofstetter to hitch up Dr. Bea's buggy and to bring it around front." Then to Bea she said, "I swear, that boy gets lazier every day. And there's no need for you and the child to wait in a cold barn when you pay good money to stable your horse. It's the least Mr. Hofstetter can do."

Bea's face felt stiff when she tried to smile. "Don't be hard on Ian. It's difficult growing into manhood." She reached out to touch her friend's arm. "If I don't make it back for the church festivities...Merry Christmas."

Bea led the child toward the boardwalk to stand in front of the door to her office. Olive called out, "Holly, Dr. Bea's Krispy Kringles are the best ever, and she puts a little magic in them, too. Merry Christmas."

Bea shook her head and sighed. How many times did she have to say that there was no magic in her cookies?

Holly looked up at her shyly. "What are Krispy Kringles?"

"Christmas cookies."

"Oh, I like cookies."

Chapter Two

Bea made certain the pinto pony was tied securely behind her buggy. She climbed in beside the little girl and snugged a heavy quilt around them, drawing the child close. For reasons she didn't fathom, Bea's motherly instinct wanted to reassure the child that her father would soon be good as new. As a doctor it was her duty to never offer false hope, especially if no hope existed. In this case, she wanted to be wrong. She clucked her faithful carriage horse into a trot.

After traveling a long distance in silence, the child spoke unexpectedly. "My mommy and baby brother went to heaven." Her voice dripped with sadness. "If my daddy goes to heaven, I'll be all alone."

Bea hugged the child a little closer. "I'm going to use all my best doctoring skills to make sure your daddy gets well."

A brutal north wind swirled, and the usually placid carriage horse shied sideways. Bea gripped the reins and spoke to calm the frightened gelding. It seemed they had traveled for a good hour. She couldn't imagine this small girl huddled next to her riding all the way to town in frigid weather to get help for her ailing father. She was brave for one so young.

"How much farther, Holly?"

The little girl leaned forward as if to see through the waning light and falling snow. "We haven't crossed the bridge yet. As soon as we do, the house is only a little ways. I set wood in the fireplace to keep Daddy warm. Maybe we'll see smoke from the chimney."

Bea doubted they'd spot chimney smoke in the fading light. She clucked the horse to a faster pace. Cold seeped through the quilt and chilled her to the bone. The child huddled against her, shivering. To comfort the child and hoping to distract her from the frigid misery, Bea asked, "Do you have a Christmas tree?"

"No, ma'am. Not since Mama died."

"How long ago was that?"

"Two years. I 'member 'cause she went to heaven when I was six and now I'm eight."

"Tell me about your mother."

"She was pretty and smelled good—like you."

For a reason that Bea couldn't fathom the compliment left her feeling lonely. "Miss Olive said you were new to Landry. Where did you live before?"

"In Cheyenne."

Compared to Landry, Cheyenne was a bustling city. Bea couldn't imagine trading modern conveniences for a small, out-of-the-way cow town. "Is there a special reason why you moved to Landry?"

Holly sniffled. "My Aunt Eloise, that's my mama's sister, wanted to take me away from my daddy. He'd have none of it. Besides, I don't like Aunt Eloise. Before Mama got sick I overheard her telling Mama that Daddy would never 'mount to a hill of beans. I don't 'xactly know what that means. Anyhow, she said it in a mean voice, so it must be bad."

"I see." Bea decided to change the subject. She turned to the child. "Have you written your letter to Santa?"

The child didn't answer, and Bea immediately regretted asking the question. She scanned the area ahead, searching for signs of chimney smoke to guide them to Holly's house.

Holly replied with an audible sigh. "Not this year. I didn't know where to send it. 'Sides, Santa probably doesn't know where I live."

No Christmas tree and no letter to Santa. Bea didn't know Tate Reed, but she was sure she was going to dislike him. No matter how much he might be grieving, it was mighty thoughtless of him to deprive his young daughter of the simple pleasure of finding gifts under a Christmas tree. She decided to rectify that. "Don't worry, Holly, I'm certain Santa will guide his sleigh to your house Christmas Eve night."

The little girl's voice was filled with uncertainty. "If he doesn't know where I live, how will he find me?"

"We'll bake Krispy Kringles. I have it on good word that Santa loves cookies, especially Krispy Kringles. We'll bake them on Christmas Eve. Once he smells them baking in the oven, he'll know where to find you."

"For real?"

"Cross my heart." Bea silently chastised herself for giving hope where there might be none.

Holly leaned out of her seat, the quilt falling from her lap. She pointed. "There, see it? The smoke. You can put the horse and buggy in the barn while I go check on Daddy."

Dark had fallen when the wagon clattered across the bridge. The old gelding picked up his pace without Bea's urging. It was as if he knew warmth lay ahead. Bea reined in the horse while Holly jumped from the buggy and ran to open the barn door. Bea said, "Go tend your father. I'll be in as soon as I take care of the horses."

Not waiting, Holly simply nodded and disappeared into the falling snow. Although the temperature in the barn was warmer than outside, Bea shivered. She made haste unhitching both horses and leading them to empty stalls. She located the feed bin and scooped a generous portion of oats. She then grabbed the quilt and her bags from the buggy and sprinted toward the house.

Pleasantly surprised by the rustic yet clean, homey interior, Bea draped the quilt over a cane-back chair. Holly called, "In here, Dr. Bea."

Bea entered the bedroom. She knew before touching the man lying there that his fever was still high. She placed a hand on his forehead. His skin was hot and dry, his cheeks gaunt with fever. His eyes fluttered. He ran his tongue over cracked and parched lips. His voice barely a whisper, he said, "Mary?"

Holly leaned on the bed. "No, Daddy. It's Doctor Bea. I brought her to make you well." The woebegone look on the child's face tugged at Bea's heart. "What's wrong with him?"

Bea lifted the man's eyelids. She opened her medical satchel and removed a stethoscope and listened to his heart and lungs. The rattle in his lungs concerned her. She folded the stethoscope and returned it to the satchel. "Your father is very sick. He has congestion in his lungs."

Tears puddled in Holly's eyes. She stammered over her next words. "I-is he g-gonna die?"

At this moment, Bea wished Tate Reed was in her small surgery where she had an ample supply of medicine. "I'll do everything in my power to help your father get well. That's all I can promise. Now, it would be most helpful if you would gather a clean nightshirt and bed sheets, and if you have them, towels and washcloths and soap, while I fill the kettle to heat water."

Tate Reed had soiled himself and needed a bath. She set about opening the buttons on his trousers. She lifted his hips as she eased the trousers down his muscular legs and hurriedly bathed his lower extremities. She covered him with a blanket and set about removing his upper garments. Once he was clean, she mixed together a poultice of mustard to place on his chest. "Holly, do you know if your father keeps whiskey in the house, and do you have any honey?"

"Yes, ma'am. I'll fetch 'em."

"I'll also need a clean jar with a lid."

While Bea waited for the water to heat, she removed a jar of mustard powder from her medical satchel and mixed the powder with flour and water to create a paste. Then she mixed a batch of honey and whiskey, which she heated and then poured into a jar.

Holly wrinkled her nose. "That yellow stuff stinks. What're you gonna do with it?"

Bea wrinkled her own nose. "The mustard plaster will draw the infection out of your father's lungs, and the whiskey and honey will quell his cough so he'll rest better." She set the medicinal aside, then filled a basin with hot water and instructed the little girl to bring the linens and clothing to the bedroom.

She thanked the child. "Holly, while I tend to your father, could you sit by the fire and write Santa a letter?"

Holly skewed her face into a frown. "I don't spell so good."

"Don't you go to school?"

The little girl hung her head until her chin almost

touched her chest. She mumbled, "No, ma'am. Daddy says it's too far for me to ride to town all by myself, and he can't take me 'cause he works."

Bea heaved an exasperated sigh. She gave the girl a quick hug. "Don't worry. Santa is very smart. All he'll ask is that you do the best you can." She lifted the basin of steaming water and carried it to the bedroom.

Holly called after her, "After you tend my daddy, can we bake cookies?"

"I'm sure it'll be past your bedtime." Bea crossed her heart and smiled. "Tomorrow we'll bake Krispy Kringles."

"Why are they called Krispy Kringles?"

"I'll tell you that tomorrow, too. Now busy yourself writing your letter, and when you're finished, come say goodnight to your father."

Chapter Three

Bea had tended many rowdy cowboys. There wasn't much of the male anatomy that she hadn't seen, as a doctor, and none had made her nervous. Yet removing Tate Reed's clothing caused her heart to flutter. She was mystified over her sudden nervousness. He was a fine-looking man. She couldn't draw her eyes away from the handsome face and the hair the color of rich maple syrup that lay on a pillow, and the way his dark lashes curled against tanned cheekbones.

Her hands trembled as she gently bathed his skin, hot and taut, the cheeks gaunt from fever, and along the strong line of his jaw and the finely etched nose and full lips. In his feverish delirium he had reached for her and as before called her—Mary. Bea assumed he thought she was his deceased wife.

Once she had completed his bath, she applied a healthy layer of mustard plaster to his chest and dressed him with a fresh nightshirt. She then applied a plaster to the soles of his feet before covering them with socks. She spooned the whiskey-laced honey into his mouth and relished the way he ran his tongue over his full lips as if savoring the cough syrup.

She brushed a burnished curl from his forehead. Giddiness welled inside her. She hadn't felt like this since her first kiss at her sweet sixteen party. *He'll take one look at me and think like all the other men in Landry.*

Besides, the man doesn't even celebrate Christmas, so stop your foolish mooning, Beata Inseldorf.

Odd she didn't know anything about Tate Reed and yet she felt drawn to him. She sighed and rationalized that he was a handsome ailing man. What she couldn't explain was the strange attachment she felt toward his child, almost as if Holly belonged to her.

Bea piled several quilts on top of Tate. The poultice would make him sweat. Sweating was good as long as he didn't get chilled. It would pull the fever and infection out of him. She gathered the soiled clothing, linens, and basin of dirty water and walked to the front door. A blast of cold air greeted her as she hastened to the end of the porch to empty the pan.

Holly sat at the table, her head bent over a piece of paper where she labored to write her letter to Santa.

"Have you had your supper, Holly?"

The child frowned at her. "I guess I forgot."

"Do you have eggs and bacon?"

"Yes, ma'am." Holly pointed. "In the cooler."

Bea bustled about the kitchen frying bacon and scrambling eggs. She reached inside her brown tote satchel and removed a tin of tea leaves. She smiled when she spied a small brown paper sack that held several peppermint sticks. Bless Olive Murphy for thinking of the child.

"Holly, would you like a cup of peppermint tea? I guarantee it will help you have sweet dreams."

Holly rewarded Bea with a dimpled smile. "Oh, yes, please. I've never had peppermint tea...ever. Aunt Eloise said tea was for grownups."

Bea hoped she never met Aunt Eloise for fear she'd give the woman a tongue lashing. "I have it on good authority that Santa's elves love peppermint tea. Of course, Santa prefers milk with his cookies." Bea broke a small piece of red-and-white goodness from the stick and used the bottom of a spoon to crush the candy into small pieces, which she added to two cups of hot tea. She then set the plates of food on the table and said, "Your father is resting, and his cough has quietened. After you finish eating, it's off to bed with you."

Holly scooped a large forkful of eggs into her mouth. She picked up the cup and blew on the steaming liquid. "Mmm, it smells good." She then savored a sip. "Yum! Will the cookies have peppermint in them?"

"No, but there is a secret ingredient." Bea smiled as she placed a finger to her lips. "You mustn't tell anyone."

Holly's eyes widened. "Oh, I won't." She finished her meal and drained the cup. Her eyes drooped as she yawned. Bea knew the child was exhausted from the long and fast-paced ride to town and with worry over her father's illness.

"Where do you sleep?"

Holly pointed to the loft. "Up there. Daddy says when he earns enough money, he'll build me a proper bedroom."

"Well, I'm certain he is a man of his word. Would you like me to brush your hair before you go to bed?"

Holly tiptoed to where her father was sleeping. She returned with a hairbrush that was inlaid with mother-of-pearl. "It was my mama's."

When she'd finished grooming the long strands of ginger-colored hair, Holly turned and thrust her arms around Bea's neck. The child clung to her, and Bea choked up. How many times had she dreamed of holding a daughter like this?

"Please don't leave us."

Bea gently loosed the little girl's arms. "I won't leave until your father is well enough to get out of bed."

"But I want you to stay."

She held Holly's hands to her breast. "I'm a doctor, and there are many sick people who need me. You understand that I have to return to town, don't you?"

The tears bubbling in the blue eyes tugged at Bea's heart. She gave Holly a hug. "Now up the ladder with you. Sweet dreams."

Bea laid two more logs on the fireplace. She brewed herself another cup of tea. When she lifted her quilt off the chair, she spied Holly's letter to Santa and carried it to the bedroom. The clock on the fireplace mantel chimed eight.

In the bedroom, she turned down the lantern until a low flame flickered, then removed the letter from her pocket. Her heart clutched as she read.

Deer Santa, my name is Holly Reed. I am eight years old and live in Landry, Wyoming. Mabee you forgot where I lived that's why you didn't come last year. Anyhow, since my mama died my daddy is always sad. Mabee next year you will bring me a dolly. I promise to be xtra good. All I want this year is for you to make my daddy happy and may-bee a Christmas tree.

A piece of Bea's heart broke when she folded the letter and tucked it into her skirt pocket. She leaned back in the rocker and closed her eyes. She needed to think of a way to bring Christmas to Holly.

Chapter Four

Bea looked at the man in the bed and thought about the little girl sleeping in the loft. She realized that what she wanted most for Christmas and the rest of her life was a husband and a child.

She sighed. Tomorrow she and Holly would bake Krispy Kringles. Christmas Eve! How could she make the child's wish come true?

For now, she needed to focus her attention on the ailing man. A coughing spell roused her from the rocker. She sat on the edge of the bed and spooned more whiskey-and-honey elixir into Tate's mouth. She wet a cloth and sponged his face and neck. He was sweating, and his breathing was no longer labored. She felt confident that by morning he'd be able to drink a cup of peppermint tea and perhaps a little solid nourishment.

The clock chimed nine. A pounding sounded at the front door. Bea gathered the shawl around her shoulders. She was hesitant to open the door. Who could be calling at this time of night?

As a matter of precaution, she grabbed the fire poker. Standing close to the door she asked, "Who's there?"

"Clive Jimson. I come to check on Tate and his daughter."

Bea opened the door. Frigid night air filled the room. "Come in, Mr. Jimson." Clouds billowed from Bea's breath as she spoke.

"Dr. Bea, what're you doing here? Who's sick…not the little girl?"

Bea placed a finger against her lips to indicate the older man should lower his voice. "It's Mr. Reed. He has a bad case of the croup." She went on to explain how Holly had ridden to town to fetch her. "What brings you to the house this time of night and in this weather?"

She invited him to sit and offered him a cup of tea. The old man said, "Yep, if'n you lace it with a shot o' whiskey. It's danged cold, if'n you'll pardon my language." He removed his gloves and wrapped his hands around the warm mug she held forward. "I got concerned. You see, Tate's been workin' fer me 'bout a year now. I give him this ol' house as part of his pay. He never misses a day…he's like clockwork. Always on time. When he didn't show, my missus got worried the little girl might be ailing." Clive chugged a healthy gulp of warm liquid. "Is there anything I can do to help with Tate?"

"Not for Mr. Reed." Excitement bubbled inside Bea. "But I'd like to share a letter with you." She removed Holly's letter from her pocket and read it to him.

"If that ain't the saddest thing ever. Plumb tugs at my heart. You know Martha and me, we lost both our young'uns to the fever. Martha never was able to have more children." Tears glistened in his aged eyes. "Tell me what I can do."

Bea collected her journal and ripped out a clean page and a pencil. She wrote out a list and handed it to him. "I would be grateful if you would ride into town and give this to Olive Murphy at the mercantile—and while she fills the order, go to my office. Upstairs in my apartment is a Christmas tree. I think it will be a nice surprise for Holly."

A wide grin lit under the old man's bushy white beard as he continued to listen to Bea's plan. "Hot dang! Pardon my language again. I can't wait to tell my Martha. It'll tickle her plumb pink. Been a long time since she's had reason to cook up a real Christmas feast." He clapped his hands together.

Bea swallowed a sudden lump in her throat. She gave him an unexpected hug, then helped him into his coat and hat. "Thank you, Mr. Jimson. This will surely be the best Christmas ever, for all of us."

After the old man left, she returned to the bedroom. Tate had thrown the covers off. She tucked the quilts in tight. His eyes opened, and he managed a weak smile. "Who are you?"

"Doctor Beata Inseldorf. Everyone calls me Dr. Bea. Are you thirsty?"

He nodded. She poured a glass of water and with one hand helped him lift his head while with the other she guided the rim to his lips. He said, "What is that terrible smell, and why are the bottoms of my feet burning?"

"It's the mustard poultices on your chest and feet to draw the inflammation from your body. If your breathing is better by morning, I'll remove them."

"Holly?"

"She's sleeping." Bea related how his daughter had bravely ridden to town seeking help. She also swallowed the harsh words building in her throat. Now wasn't the time to chastise a man who still might die if she couldn't keep the fever and the inflammation in his lungs at bay.

"So, what's the verdict? Will I live through the night?" He tried to laugh but ended up with another coughing spasm.

She realized he had no idea how ill he was. Without saying anything, she reached for her stethoscope and listened to his racing heart. She moved it slowly over his chest to listen to his lungs. She was satisfied the gurgling had stopped, a good sign the fluid was dissipating. "I'll do my best to see that you're still here to celebrate Christmas."

She filled a spoon with laudanum. "Open wide."

"What is it?"

"Laudanum. It will ease the pain in your chest and help you rest."

His voice rasped, "Yeah, I know what it is. Had my share during the war, when I was shot." He grimaced as the bitter liquid slid down his throat. "We don't do Christmas."

Bea straightened her shoulders. She didn't have any magic words to help him forget a dark period in his life. She arched an eyebrow and offered a sly smile. "You will this year. I promised Holly, and I never go back on a promise."

****

Christmas Eve Morning

Tate opened his eyes. As his vision cleared, fatigue rode him hard, and for a moment he didn't remember getting sick and didn't know how long he'd slept.

Holly!

What had happened to his daughter? He tried to sit up but fell back, unable to lift himself off the bed. His vision went all blurry, and the room spun out of control. He lay still, trying to regain his sense of balance. When his vision cleared, he focused on the woman sleeping in the rocking chair next to his bed. Her hair had tumbled out of her chignon and settled around her shoulders like a blonde cape. She was lovely, her complexion creamy-smooth, with a deep blush to her cheeks and her lips a lush pink. She looked too elegant for this rough-hewn house. He thought she looked serene in her slumber. Not a woman of extraordinary beauty like his Mary, but still beautiful. Something about her appealed to him strongly. Maybe it was the way she'd taken calm control during his coughing spell or how her face had softened when she spoke of his daughter. What was her name? Oh, yes, Dr. Bea. She had a sweet, loving face.

He lay back, exhausted. Before he drifted off to sleep, he remembered Dr. Bea saying something about Christmas. Christmas was a fairy tale. The specialness of the holiday had died when he'd buried his wife and infant son on Christmas Eve two years ago. He lay there thinking of a thousand excuses to avoid the holiday and especially the disappointment in his young daughter's eyes.

Tate wrestled with his thoughts. When sleep did revisit, he was disturbed by dreams of his wife. He worried that he was holding on to her to avoid falling in love again. It was true he had built a living tomb around himself and was slowly drying up inside.

Bea Inseldorf had lit a small spark of life in him, and he wasn't certain whether he was glad or frustrated. He didn't know how he felt or what he wanted to do about it—what he wanted to do about his bewildering feelings for the beautiful doctor. Being sick and lying in bed would certainly force him to come up with some answers.

He awoke to a tantalizing aroma.

Chapter Five

Morning arrived with a flurry of excitement, perfect for Christmas Eve. Bea opened the bedroom door and motioned for Holly. Tate had awakened long enough for her to spoon-feed him a cup of beef broth. His fever had broken during the night. She had removed the poultices and given him a warm sponge bath. Holly perched on the side of his bed. She placed her tiny hand on his whiskered cheek. She looked up at Bea, tears glistening on the fringes of her lashes. "You saved my daddy."

She jumped up and grabbed Bea around the waist and hugged her so hard Bea grunted. The genuine warmth in the child's hug took Bea by surprise, but it was the look in Tate's eyes that tripped her heart. It was as if something connected them so that every emotion he felt touched her in some way. Every nerve in her body hummed. If she didn't know better, she'd swear she was coming down with a fever.

She gathered the cup and spoon as she stammered, "I promised Holly we'd bake cookies."

"Yes, Daddy, Krispy Kringles. Mrs. Murphy at the mercantile said Dr. Bea puts magic in them. We're making them for Santa Claus."

"Holly!" Tate's voice was stern.

Whatever quixotic emotion had passed between them vanished. Bea refused to allow Tate Reed to spoil his daughter's Christmas. "Your father needs to rest."

She arched a brow as she held out her hand to the child and smiled. "Come, we have lots of cookies to bake."

Bea soon forgot about Tate's surliness. She showed Holly how to break the eggs into a bowl and beat them into a froth. Holly poured the measured sugar into the egg mixture. "Dr. Bea, why are the cookies called Krispy Kringles?"

Bea blended the sugar and butter together. "Well, my mother and father were from a country far across the sea called Germany. German children call Santa Claus 'Kris Kringle,' and they know the jolly old man loves cookies. One year, a terrible blizzard covered the entire country with snow. Most of the menfolk were away at sea, leaving the village with mostly women and children. The villagers feared Kris Kringle and his reindeer wouldn't be able to see their chimney smoke to deliver toys to the children. One widowed mother decided her four young children had suffered enough sadness. So she braved the cold and trudged through the snow from house to house, knocking on doors, inviting each mother and grandmother to come to her small cottage. She had a plan to save Christmas. The widow's husband had been a sailor, and on one of his voyages, before he was lost at sea, he visited places called the Spice Islands and Malaysia, where he traded barrels of salted fish for containers of nutmeg and black pepper. The widow swore that she had a secret ingredient guaranteed to create an aroma so sweet and so strong that Santa would follow his nose to each of their houses."

Her eyes filled with amazement, Holly stared up at Bea. "Did it work?"

Bea reached inside her tote bag and withdrew a small silver tin. She carefully opened the lid, and before adding a healthy pinch of the burnished powder to the batter she said, "Smell, then tell me what you think."

A smile lit the child's face. "Mm. I think Santa will find his way to my house tonight. But you still didn't tell me how the cookie got its name."

Bea also removed a sack of shelled pecans from her bag. She wrapped the nuts in a cloth and showed Holly how to use a rolling pin to crush them. While she added the nuts, the nutmeg, and some black pepper to the batter, Bea said, "Legend has it that when the jolly old man asked the name of the cookies, the young widow spoke up and said, 'Krispy Kringles.' "

"That's the bestest story ever." Holly furrowed her brow. "What was the young widow's name?"

Bea smiled. "Her name was Helga Inseldorf." The amazed expression on the child's face prompted Bea to say, "She was my great-great-grandmother."

So engrossed were they in setting the cookies in the oven and then crushing sugar into powdery granules to use on the baked cookies, neither Bea nor Holly were aware that Tate stood in his bare feet, gripping the bedroom door. A creak alerted Bea.

Tate managed to say, "Something smells good. I thought... I thought..."

Bea grabbed Tate before he slid to the floor. He was so close. His eyes. His lips. Her gaze locked on his mouth. His lips were full and firm. Even through two days' growth of whiskers, the cleft in his chin was obvious. His cheek bones were chiseled. Her gaze floated to his eyes. Brown like freshly brewed coffee. She could easily fall in love with this man. She must be losing her mind. How could she love a man who deprived his child of the joys of Christmas?

He rasped, "Don't be filling my daughter's head with fairytale nonsense."

She managed to get him back to bed, where she covered his shivering body with a quilt. Holly followed her. "It's not a fairytale, Daddy." She sniffled. "You'll see. Dr. Bea promised."

The sound of jingling bells broke the tension and wiped away the disappointment on Holly's face. She raced to the great room, while Bea scowled down at Tate. Her only words were, "Shame on you."

She sniffed the air. "Holly, take the cookies out of the oven before they burn."

A loud knock sounded against the door, followed by Clive Jimson's voice shouting, "Merry Christmas!"

Bea opened the door to find a plump woman with a pleasant smile standing next to the portly man holding the small decorated yule tree from her apartment. She placed a finger to her lips. The woman whispered, "Oh, Clive has already told me." She stuck out a hand. "We haven't officially met. I'm Martha, this ol' coot's wife. I've brought a couple of jars of chicken broth for Tate."

Bea thanked the woman and invited her in.

Holly set the pan of cookies on the table. A wide grin lit her face. She squealed with delight. She clapped her hands together. "A Christmas tree! It's beautiful. Is it for me?"

Mr. Jimson laughed a jolly laugh. "I have it on good word that Santa got your letter and asked me to bring this Christmas tree to you. I'll set it right here in front of the window."

Holly skipped about, giggling and clapping her hands. Martha Jimson asked, "What is that wonderful smell?"

"Krispy Kringles. We baked them so Santa can find my house." Holly shot Bea a conspiratorial look. "Dr. Bea puts a secret 'gredient in them." And then she said, "Can we have one now?"

The warm aroma of vanilla and nutmeg filled the house. "Of course, and take one to your father. But first you must roll them in the powdered sugar. That will help the cookies melt in your mouth."

Holly dusted the cookies, licking the sugar from her fingers afterward. While she was out of the room, Bea bustled about pouring coffee. Martha exclaimed she'd never tasted a better cookie. "What is it that leaves a little spicy bite on the end of my tongue?"

"That's one of the secret ingredients." Bea wasn't about to share all her secrets.

While Holly was out of earshot, Clive excused himself. He whispered, "I'll just leave *the you-know-whats* in the woodbin, Dr. Bea. There's no need for you to traipse to the barn in knee-deep snow in the dark." His gloved hand on the door latch, he winked. "And Mrs. Murphy put a little something extra in for Holly."

"I think I'm as excited as she is." Bea took the chair on the opposite side of the table.

Martha asked about Tate. "I hope he's well enough to sit at the table tomorrow. I've got a turkey roasting, and cornbread dressing, and sweet yams, and—"

Bea interrupted. "My goodness, there's no need for you to go to all that trouble. I'm sure there's food in the larder I can cook."

Martha brushed crumbs and sugar from her shawl. She reached for another cookie. "Nonsense, it's been a long time since I've had the pleasure of preparing a Christmas feast. But if you would like to put together a soup, that would be wonderful, and perhaps hot chocolate for later."

Clive stamped snow off his boots. He stood before the potbellied stove to warm his hands. "Think I'll take a look-see at Tate to see how he's holdin' up, while you ladies confab a bit." He winked at his wife.

After the Jimsons left for home and the last batch of cookies was cooling, Bea said, "While your father is resting, would you like to go outside and build a snowman?"

At the child's delight, Bea suggested they bundle up against the cold. Neither she nor Holly were aware that Tate stood at the window watching them as they rolled balls of snow and fashioned a snowman, and neither had any way of knowing the smile that crinkled his eyes.

Chapter Six

For a long time Tate lay staring up at the ceiling. His conversation with Clive Jimson played around inside his mind, and now his conscience bothered him. Mary had always said his greatest failing was not being gifted with words. *I swear, Tate Reed, your tongue would shrivel up and fall out of your mouth before you paid me a compliment.* Those words haunted him. He'd never told her how much he loved her, and now he'd never have the chance.

One thing for certain—he'd try to do better by Holly. She was a mini-image of her mother, and she needed to know she was the most precious person in his life. *I know working hard every day to provide for us is your way of showing us how much you care.* He remembered the tears that brimmed in the blue eyes that reminded him of spring water when Mary had gone on to say, *but Holly and I need to hear the words—I love you. It's just three little words, Tate. Why are they so difficult for you to say?*

In all the times he'd put Holly to bed, he couldn't remember holding her hand, or kissing her goodnight, and worse, he couldn't remember if he'd comforted her after he'd buried her mother and baby brother.

In the past few days, he'd found out things about himself that he didn't like, and worse, the things he was missing.

And all because of Dr. Bea Inseldorf, a woman who represented everything he'd lost. He wasn't blind. It was plain that she and Holly had a deep affection for each other. Plus they had gotten a lot done in the past couple of days. Bea had dusted and swept, while Holly helped cook and wash the dishes, and Bea had even milked the cow and fed the livestock—things Mary had considered beneath her so-called social upbringing.

Voices interrupted his musing. Bea was saying, "Off to bed with you. Santa can't come if you aren't asleep."

"But I'm not sleepy, Dr. Bea."

"You've had a long day baking cookies and building a snowman, plus helping me with the chores."

Tate tiptoed to the bedroom door and opened it a mere crack. Bea had tweaked his daughter's cheek. She said, "Remember, Santa knows when you're sleeping, and he knows when you're awake. So for goodness' sake, you don't want him to fly over your house and keep on flying, do you?"

Holly's eyes widened. Her little mouth formed an Oh. "No, ma'am."

Bea smiled as she handed the child a plate. "Put a few cookies on the plate and set them next to the Christmas tree. I'll pour a cup of milk."

Holly obeyed without protest. Bea added, "Tell your father goodnight, and then off you go to put on your nightie. I'll come up and hear your prayer."

Tate tried to suppress the cough. A spasm overtook him as he hurried to bed and pulled the quilt up to his chin. By the time Bea followed Holly into the room, his chest heaved as he gasped for air.

Once Holly had told him a quick goodnight and gone to her bed, Bea addressed him. Although her voice was rich and warm, her words were spoken in a sharp tone. She reached for the jar of elixir. "Shame on you for eavesdropping on our conversation, and in your bare feet, no less, and on a cold floor." She scowled as she dipped the spoon into the amber liquid. "Open wide."

Even though his teeth chattered, and he still suffered from fatigue, Tate was amazed to discover that his blood was still capable of rushing quick and hot through his veins as she bent close to shove a spoonful of honey-laced whiskey into his mouth. His belly drew taut with a delicious ache that had nothing to do with cough medicine.

Their gazes, hers cornflower blue and his coffee brown, slammed into each other. She stood abruptly and stepped away from the bed. Her voice quivered when she said, "Are you hungry?"

His body wound tight, his voice failed him. He cleared his throat and managed to rasp, "I could go for a cup of coffee and a couple of those delicious cookies."

"I'll bring you a cup of tea brewed with special herbs to hold your fever at bay. It's not particularly pleasing to the taste. At least the Krispy Kringles will make the tea more palatable." The way her hips swayed as she walked to the door filled him with a myriad of erotic emotions.

He forced his mind to shift directions. Mary and the infant's death had been painful. He wondered if they would have stayed together if the baby had lived? His life with Mary, and without her, had taught him an unforgettable lesson. It made him realize that he valued the idea of long-term relationships.

Even as he closed his eyes he envisioned holding Bea in his arms, making love to her, marriage with her.

He huffed out a breath at the thought.

She leaned over him and touched his forehead. "Are you having difficulty breathing?"

He needed to rein in all this unlikely speculation. The lantern light played nicely off the curves of her lovely face. He scooted to a sitting position, and as if his lips had a mind of their own, he took her by the arms and kissed her. To his surprise, she responded.

She gasped and stepped away from the bed. A hand to her lips, she stammered, "You are awfully bold for an ailing man."

He frowned. In a few short days, this quiet miracle of a woman had transformed his life. He wanted to tell her how much that meant to him. He would when the time was right.

****

Bea was glad tomorrow was Christmas, and while she hated to leave Holly, she was ready to leave this house, to leave Tate Reed, to leave the odd emotions he evoked in her, and return to town, to her office and patients, to reality.

She did her best not to be affected by the way Tate's focused attention made her insides tingle. A gust of wind rattled the windows despite the fact that she had latched them tight to protect the glass panes. This bit of distraction chased away the peculiar physical reaction she had to her close proximity to Tate's well-defined handsomeness.

Once the herbal brew was sufficiently steeped, she poured the steaming liquid into a mug and with that and a plate of cookies returned to the bedroom. She hesitated to help Tate to a sitting position for fear he'd kiss her again—and for fear of her reaction. His hand brushed hers as she reached out to hand him the cup of tea and cookies. He said, "Thank you." His words were smooth as he met her eyes with a ready smile.

Her lips twitched, but she chose not to respond. For a good length of time they sat in an awkward silence. She had never been so aware of another person in her entire life. She seemed to feel every shift of his body against the bed's headboard, every turn of his head when he looked in her direction. Despite her hyperawareness, it jolted her a little when his words broke the silence.

"I don't apologize for kissing you."

He polished off the last Krispy Kringle, savoring the unusual but pleasant aftertaste. That's when it occurred to him that he wanted a wife, a family, and roots…a real home.

****

Even though he didn't know Bea, he realized he wanted her to be part of his life. Much to his dismay, he felt a deep connection to her. As before, she slept in the rocking chair in case he needed her during the night. Before retiring, she had banked a fire in the fireplace. The flickering flames cast a golden glow over Bea's delicate features.

As if sensing his gaze, she opened her eyes and regarded him through a ring of dark lashes. "Are you having difficulty breathing?"

Embarrassed to be caught staring, he shrugged. "I was just wondering what made you decide to become a doctor."

A gentle smile curved her lips, as if recalling the past brought her pleasure. "My father was a maker of cheese, and my mother was a doctor. They were the perfect imperfect couple. When I wasn't helping my father, I often assisted mother, even before I went away to medical school. Being a doctor just seemed a natural path for me. I love what I do and can't imagine doing anything else."

"Is your father living?"

Bea sighed. "Sadly, he died when I was about fifteen."

"You looked sad just now when you spoke of your mother."

"She passed last year. This is my first Christmas without her. I miss her terribly."

"I know the feeling."

"Holly told me about her mother and baby brother. Is that why you don't celebrate Christmas?"

His face flushed red, and it wasn't from a rising fever. It was the eve before Christmas, and all he wanted was to be left alone with his misery.

"Daddy...Dr. Bea?" Holly rubbed sleepy eyes as she wandered into the bedroom.

Tate thought she looked so small as she stood next to the open door. She just stood there until Bea said, "I'm sorry, Holly. I didn't mean to forget." She rose from the rocker and extended her hand. "Come, I'll tuck you in."

As Bea led the child from the room, Holly turned and offered a limp smile. "I'm glad you ate the Krispy Kringles, Daddy. Mrs. Murphy at the mercantile said Dr. Bea puts magic in them."

He rested his head on the pillow again and told himself to forget his fanciful notions. Bea Inseldorf was a beautiful, educated woman, a doctor. What had she just said about her parents? The perfect imperfect couple. "I've never much believed in magic. But maybe Holly is right. Maybe there is magic in your cookies."

33

From the withering expression Bea wore on her face when she returned to the room, Tate half expected her to slap him. Instead she lit into him like a raging storm. "Mr. Reed, you are a selfish, cold-hearted man. How dare you take away that sweet child's joy simply because you've decided to shrivel up and clomp around like a living dead person! Whether you like it or not, I promised that beautiful little girl a happy Christmas, and like I said before, I never break a promise."

When he tried to interrupt, she held out her hand like a stop signal and continued, "Earlier you asked why you stunk. Well, I've changed my mind. It's not the mustard poultice that you smelled. Oh, no! It's you rotting from the inside out because you've chosen to wallow in the mulligrubs."

Though she worked to keep her voice lowered, it continued to rise in a harsh whisper. "Have you no care in your soul for that sweet child whose only wish for Christmas is for Santa Claus to make her daddy happy?"

Bea pulled the letter from her apron pocket and plopped it on Tate's chest. She grabbed the quilt from the back of the rocker and wrapped it around her shoulders. "Your fever has broken, and your lungs are clear. When that precious child wakes up in the morning to see what's under the tree, if you have an iota of caring in your heart, I beg you, please don't spoil her joy, even if you have to plaster on a fake smile."

She strode to the door. Tate said, "Where are you going?"

"To play Santa Claus."

Without taking his eyes off her, he reached for the lantern to turn up the flame and then opened the folded piece of paper. His heart thudded against his chest, and a large lump in his throat threatened to choke him as he read his daughter's simple request—*Make my daddy smile again.*

Chapter Seven

Shivering beneath the quilt, Bea was grateful that Mr. Jimson had left the packages inside the woodbin. She grabbed the basket of gifts and hastened to the house's warmth. With loving hands she placed a porcelain doll with blonde curls and adorned in a blue silk dress under the tree. She wanted the lifelike toy to be the first thing Holly spotted when she climbed down the loft's ladder. Bea set three additional gaily wrapped gifts under the tree. One she knew was an illustrated copy of *Black Beauty*. After all, what little girl wouldn't love a storybook about horses. Although the other two presents were a mystery, she was certain one was from Olive Murphy and the other perhaps from Clive and Martha Jimson. A smile broadened Bea's face when she lifted a small box wrapped in green velvet paper with her name neatly penned on a tag. She recognized the handwriting as that of her friend Olive.

Still angry, Bea warmed the cup of milk Holly had set out for Santa. She sprinkled a bit of nutmeg over the top and sat at the table, enjoying the cookies that went with it. She changed into her nightgown and returned to the bedroom. She placed a log inside the fireplace and stirred the embers before settling in the rocking chair.

Silence filled the room. As she bent to turn out the lantern's flame, Tate's voice startled her. He said, "How does a beautiful and spirited woman like you escape from being snapped up?"

Bea was tempted to tell him it was none of his business. She thought she should offer him an apology for her irate outburst, instead she said, "I suppose the timing has never been right."

He held up the open letter. His eyes clouded with hurt. "I've always been a man of few words. I think the words inside my head. I just can't seem to get them to come out of my mouth."

Bea gave him a puzzled look. "I don't understand."

"You're right about me being selfish and shriveling up and dying. I didn't realize it until you so sharply pointed it out."

Tate gathered the blanket around him and swung his long legs over the side of the bed to sit on the edge. He stared into the flickering flames. Bea watched the shadows cast by the firelight dance across his face like so many devils. Instinct told her to remain silent, that he wanted to talk. She waited.

He cleared his throat. "I didn't deserve Mary. She was beautiful and educated and could have had the pick of any man in all of West Virginia. I'm not sure why she married me." He shifted on the bed and sighed. "Maybe to make Willard Stiles jealous." He racked a hand through his dark hair. "Willard was everything I wasn't. He was a lawyer. I was a coal miner. He was spit and polish." Tate shrugged. "No matter how much I washed, there was always coal dirt on me."

He continued to stare into the fire. Bea waited. He began again. "Eloise—that's Mary's sister—had wed Fred Stiles. Fred and Willard were lawyers in their father's law office. Fred had aspirations to become a senator. He and Eloise moved to Cheyenne, where he established himself and began his trip into politics. Eloise begged Mary to divorce me and marry Willard and follow them to Wyoming. By that time, Mary was pregnant with Holly. So Eloise promised Fred would get me a good paying job and even provide a place to live if we moved."

Silence.

Bea prompted, "Did he?"

"What?"

"Did your brother-in-law get you a job?"

Tate was quiet as if weighing his answer. "No. Not at first. Stubborn pride kept me in the mine. Mary refused to live in the shanties provided to the workers and their families. Heck, I could barely afford more than a room in the boarding house. I knew she was miserably unhappy. How could she not be, when every day she saw Willard's wife prancing around in expensive dresses and practically thumbing her nose at Mary. After Holly was born, Mary...withheld herself from me. I worked overtime to earn enough money to buy passage to Wyoming. All I wanted was to show my wife how much I loved her."

He sighed as if his heart was heavy. "Fred hired me. I worked as his office lackey, and he never missed a chance to remind me daily that I *owed* him. We even lived on the third floor of his and Eloise's mansion. Every Christmas was a big whoop-de-do. It didn't matter what I gave Mary. It never lived up to what Fred had given Eloise. It was the happiest two years of Mary's life."

Bea forced a smile. "What about you?"

Tate's reply came out sounding hoarse. "Mary opened up, gave herself to me. Yes, I guess in a

38

complacent sort of way I was happy."

"Holly said the reason you left Cheyenne is because her Aunt Eloise wanted to take her away from you."

He cleared his throat and answered quietly. "Mary's labor started prematurely. She suffered two days of agony. Sometimes I can still hear her screams. The baby, a little boy, was awfully tiny when he finally came. He didn't live long enough to draw a good breath, and Mary had lost so much blood that..." His voice hitched. "Instead of opening presents and rejoicing on Christmas Day, I buried my wife and son.

"Mary wasn't even cold in the grave when Eloise handed me a document stating that she was to have full guardianship of my daughter if anything were to happen to Mary, because I wasn't fit to raise my child. That was two years ago."

Bea dashed away angry tears. "Is that why you never come to town?"

He nodded. "There was no future in the coal mines, and I had no family left in the Appalachians. I was down to my last dime when my wagon wheel broke and left us stranded in the middle of nowhere. I wasn't even sure where we were. All I wanted was to get as far away from Cheyenne as possible. If I didn't go to town and no one knew my name, the law wouldn't be able to find me.

"Thank the lucky stars Clive Jimson came along. Long story short—he gave me a job and, as part of my pay, this house. It was his and Martha's when they first married."

Tate lay back and closed his eyes. Bea rose to pull the quilt over him and bent to tuck it around him. Her heart overflowed with compassion for Tate. She'd had no right to judge him.

Chapter Eight

"Dr. Bea?"

"Yes, Mr. Reed?"

"Do you think running away with my daughter as opposed to letting her live with Eloise and Fred was selfish of me?"

"I think if you had left Holly, both of you would be miserable for the rest of your lives." She thought for a moment. He didn't want to lose his child. Her heart overflowed with compassion for a man forced by circumstances to kidnap the one person he loved most in the world. "But—"

He sensed her hesitation. "As long as we're being open and honest, go ahead. I'm man enough to hear the rest of what you have to say."

She didn't mean to speak with harsh undertones to her voice. Perhaps that's why she was an old maid. Men didn't admire women who freely spoke their minds. She tried to soften her voice. "You have admitted that you say certain words in your mind but can't get them out of your mouth. Mr. Reed... Tate... Is the reason you don't express your feelings because you've been taught that it isn't manly?"

There, she had said the words he probably didn't want to hear, and she mentally berated herself for having such an honest tongue.

He opened his mouth to contradict her. It was

something of an irritation that she had used his words to make a point. He couldn't seem to take his eyes off this beautiful woman. He couldn't help but wonder what it would be like to have her as a wife. She was everything Mary had never been. He chastised himself. *Stop being delusional. You've only known this woman a few days. Love at first sight, like the magic in her cookies, is a myth.*

He snorted in contempt. Bea apparently mistook his reaction. She said, "I apologize. There are times when my tongue seems to override the sensible side of my brain." She stepped away from the bed to the rocking chair. "I'm here if you need me."

He rolled to his side and faced the wall. The fever had left him. It would take a while before he regained his strength. Like it or not, he no longer needed her as a doctor. He knew she would leave. After all, she had other patients to tend. He guessed she would leave the day after Christmas, or perhaps even Christmas Day, after the festivities.

In such a short time she had become an important part of Holly's life—and, truth be known, his also. Intellectually, he'd always known her presence was temporary, but his heart would have none of it. She had filled an empty space inside him. How had he fallen in love with a woman he knew would walk out of his life just as suddenly as she had walked into it?

****

Bea wasn't sure what had disturbed her dream. Perhaps it was Tate shifting position in the bed. At a shuffling sound, she opened her eyes to mere slits. Except for the red embers in the fireplace, the room was dark. Maybe a rat had found a way into the room. She disliked vermin of any type. She ever so slightly turned her head and swallowed back the gasp when she realized the hulking dark figure was Tate. He was squatting at the end of the bed. Her vision acclimated to the room's dim interior. He leaned over an open chest. She watched him gently close the top and shove the chest under the bed. That solved the mystery of the shuffling sound. No vermin!

The beats of her heart rose in her throat when he came to stand in front of her. She continued to peer through slit eyes. When he leaned forward she was certain he might kiss her. She wasn't sure if it was disappointment or relief she felt when he turned and eased across the room. He opened the bedroom door, letting in a draft of cold air.

Curiosity wanted to know why Tate was wandering about in bare feet and a nightshirt. Common sense kept her rooted to the rocking chair.

The clock chimed four times. It was too early to rise. Tate re-entered the room and eased down on the bed. She watched and listened until his breathing evened out and she knew he'd drifted into a peaceful sleep.

Her body ached from the long nights of sitting in the rocker. She missed the comfort of her goose-down mattress and yearned for a long, hot soak in her clawfoot tub. She wriggled to ease the discomfort in her back.

Her mind filled with thoughts. Except for her years at medical college, she had lived her entire life in Landry. She knew the people. She had a place in the community. Tate lived ten miles from town, too far for her to make daily trips to where patients could easily come to her office, and then there were her dreams of building a hospital. The thought of moving to this remote two-room house worried her.

Besides, she didn't know the first thing about being a mother to an eight-year-old girl, plus she wanted other children. How could she manage a family and a medical practice? Her mother had done both, though, so why couldn't she?

The thought shocked her, and she gasped out loud. She loved Holly and didn't want to leave her. Had she fallen in love with Tate, too? Not in just a few days. The thought quite literally shocked her.

No, she was in love with a dream. It was the magic of the Krispy Kringles that had her thinking like a foolish schoolgirl. She rose and walked over to the window. Snow continued to feather down. The land was completely white and silent. A Christmas fairyland.

Life was complicated. A wave of sadness swept over Bea. Tomorrow, after Christmas dinner, she would announce her departure.

Chapter Ten

"He came…he came! Wake up…Daddy…Dr. Bea. Come look what Santa left under the tree."

The clock chimed seven times.

Bea couldn't believe she had overslept. She grabbed her shawl and wrapped it around her shoulders. "Are you awake, Mr. Reed?"

He sat on the edge of the bed and yawned. "I wish you would call me Tate."

She smiled and nodded. "Merry Christmas, Tate."

He returned her smile. "I think we should go see what all the excitement is about."

Standing next to the tree, Holly hugged the porcelain doll to her chest. Tate gave Bea a questioning look. She merely lifted her eyebrows, and said to the little girl, "You have to give her a name."

"I think I'll call her Princess."

"It's a perfect name," Tate said. "Before you get busy with your other presents, I have a gift for you."

Holly's eyes widened. "For me…truly?"

Tate reached in among the little tree's branches and withdrew a small red velvet bag pulled shut with a thin gold cord. He handed it to Holly.

She carefully opened the bag, reached in, and removed a necklace. A gold cross dangled from the filigree gold chain. Her face was filled with surprise and awe at such a gift. "This is for me?"

44

Tate took it from her hands. He lifted her long brown hair and placed the necklace around his daughter's neck. "It was your mother's. She wanted you to have it when you were old enough. I think she'd agree that you're old enough."

Bea's eyes misted when Holly flung her arms around Tate's neck, and he didn't hesitate to return the embrace. Holly kissed him on the cheek. "May I open the rest of my presents?"

Tate nodded.

Holly lifted another gift. She looked up and smiled. "It's from Dr. Bea." She was careful not to tear the colorful green foiled paper. Her smile assured Bea that she had made the right choice when Holly hugged her. "Thank you. I love horses."

Holly set the book aside as if it were a national treasure. She lifted another present. "This one is from Mr. Clive and Miz Martha."

Tate said, "Why don't you wait until they arrive? I'm sure it'd please them to watch you open it."

Without argument the child set the large package back under the tree. She said, "There's one more, and it has your name on it, Dr. Bea." She offered a puzzled look as she continued, "I'm glad we made a whole bunch of Krispy Kringles, 'cause he left you a present, too." And then she urged Bea to hurry and open the gift.

"Who is *he*?" asked Tate.

"Oh, Daddy, Kris Kringle, of course. That's what the children in Germany call him." She scrunched her face. "I kinda like that name. If I ever get a reindeer, I'm gonna name him Kris Kringle."

Bea and Tate's laughter filled the room. She opened the gift that she knew had to be from Olive. The square green box held the cameo brooch that Bea had taken in several weeks ago to have the broken clasp replaced.

Holly leaned over to look. "It's beautiful. Did Kris Kringle bring it?"

Bea's voice quivered. It took several minutes to clear the tears building in her throat. "In a way, he did, Holly."

"Why are you crying when you should be happy?"

Bea brushed away a tear that trailed down her cheek. Holly went to sit on her father's lap.

Bea said, "These are happy tears. You see, my mother received her angel wings last year. This is my first Christmas without her." Bea lovingly held the cameo to her breast. "This was my great-grandmother's. She gave it to my mother, and now it belongs to me. The clasp was broken, and someone repaired it. Now I can wear it."

"Will you give it to your little girl someday?"

It was an innocent question. Bea looked at Tate and thought he looked at her as if she were his favorite cookie. His expression almost caused her to laugh. "If I ever marry and have a daughter, yes, the brooch will be hers."

"What if you don't? Marry, I mean, and have a little girl?"

"Holly Reed!" Tate chastised.

"It's an honest question, Tate." Bea sighed. She thought for a moment. Holly would be the closest she would ever come to having a daughter. "Then I will give it to you. But you must promise to take good care of it and then pass it on to your daughter."

Tate rose. "I'm a bit tired of wearing a nightshirt. If you'll excuse me, I'll get dressed."

"Oh, no," Holly cried. "I'm sorry, Daddy."

He knelt and took her hands. "Sorry for what?"

Concern shadowed the child's face. She glanced at Bea. "I forgot to ask Kris Kringle to bring daddy a gift."

Tate hugged his daughter. "He, that is, Kris Kringle, did bring me something—something money can't buy." Bea knew by the expression on his face that he struggled to get the words out. She offered him an encouraging smile and a reassuring nod.

Tate's chest heaved a deep sigh. "He brought me a house filled with love, a beautiful daughter, and Dr. Bea to make me well."

"Oh, Daddy, you ate a whole bunch of Krispy Kringles, and everybody knows Dr. Bea puts magic in them."

With that Bea said, "I think it's time for you and me to get dressed, young lady." She smiled at Tate. "I hope you're hungry, because I'm in the mood for biscuits and gravy."

He agreed as he lifted the remaining cookie from the plate next to the Christmas tree. "Here's to a Krispy Kringle Christmas. While you ladies get dressed, I'll brew the coffee."

"It's Christmas, Daddy. Can I have coffee, too?"

He tweaked her nose. "Only because it's a special day, and you can only have it with extra milk. I don't want your growth stunted."

Bea left the room. When she returned, her blonde hair was fashioned in a neat chignon. She wore a white apron to protect the green dress she had hastily packed with no thought of Christmas at the time. Father and daughter sat at the table sipping coffee. The short hemline on Holly's faded blue gingham dress denoted how long it had been since the child had a new garment. Bea vowed to change that.

****

While Bea and Holly prepared breakfast, Tate lifted a large kettle of water from the stove. He returned to the bedroom, where he bathed and afterward trimmed his scraggly beard. He wet a comb and tried to tame his unruly hair. Dressed in a clean shirt and tan chino trousers, he inhaled the aroma of bacon and biscuits. When he returned to the great room, there was a beauty and warmth that surrounded everything. The sight of Bea bending to lift a pan of biscuits from the oven made him realize he was hungry for more than food. He worked to quell the lump rising inside his long johns.

It was Christmas Day, and though he hadn't fully regained his strength, he felt more alive than he had in years. Bea stood at the stove, looking more beautiful than a woman had the right to look. His heart practically flipped over when she turned, smiled, and motioned him to the table.

Over breakfast, Bea talked about the town's decorations. "Every store is decorated on the inside and out, and fresh juniper branches fill the air with a wonderful fragrance."

Holly clapped her hands and giggled. "I bet their Christmas trees aren't as pretty as ours."

After breakfast and with the dishes washed, Tate helped Bea peel potatoes and onions while his daughter sat in a chair having a pretend conversation with her new doll. Once the potato soup was simmering, Bea declared that to truly enjoy the rest of Christmas Day, they should all take a nap before the Jimsons arrived.

Chapter Ten

Christmas afternoon brought the sound of sleigh bells and snorting horses. Holly ran to the window. "They're here!"

Tate grabbed his slicker hanging from a hook attached to the door.

Bea fisted her hands on her hips. "Oh, no, you don't. I didn't sit up with you all these many nights to have your fever return. Mr. Jimson can take care of his own horses."

Bea moistened her lips, drawing his attention to the sensual curve of her smile. He inhaled a shaky breath. "Yes, ma'am."

A knock rapped on the door. Bea rolled her eyes and afforded Tate a quick smile before she opened the door.

Clive Jimson helped his wife up the steps. He stamped snow from his boots. Spotting Tate, he declared, "It's good to see ya up and 'bout. I was 'fraid I might lose the best handyman I've had in a long time."

Handyman. The word stung. A coal miner, office lackey, and now a handyman. He had little to offer any woman. He needed to get the notion of marriage out of his mind.

Tate relieved the old man of the four straw baskets laden with food, while Bea helped Martha remove layers of wraps.

Tate set the baskets on the table. "Bea is a fine

doctor."

Holly snuggled against her father. "Don't forget the magic 'gredient in the Krispy Kringles, Daddy. That helped too."

Bea waved her hand as if shooing away the compliment. She felt the blush crawling up her neck. She said, "The two of you must be chilled to the bone. How about a cup of potato soup to warm you up?" She added, "Martha, you've brought enough food to feed an army."

The older woman's eyes twinkled. "I don't imagine the leftovers will go to waste. We'll just leave them here for Tate and…my goodness, child, I don't believe I've ever seen a prettier dolly."

Holly cradled the doll. "Her name is Princess, and Santa Claus brought her." She also showed off her necklace and book before she cut her eyes toward the tree. "There's 'nother present under the tree. Daddy said I had to wait 'til you and Mr. Clive came so you can see me open it."

Clive pulled out a chair for his wife. He chose a chair next to her. Bea ladled five cups of soup and brought them to the table. Martha said, "It's been a long time since Clive and I have watched children open gifts. You go right ahead, child."

Tate nodded toward his daughter. She said, "Here, Daddy, hold Princess."

All eyes were on the little girl as she removed the paper. Her lips widened into a dimpled smile as she unfolded a pink apron with white tatting around the edges, her name neatly embroidered in blue letters across the bib. "It has my name on it, and a pocket, too." She rewarded Martha and Clive with hugs.

She retrieved the doll from her father and then asked

him to tie the apron around her waist.

"Say, this here is mighty fine tater soup," Clive said. "Near as good as them cookies. I shor'ly hope you got 'nough left for us to nibble on."

Bea gathered the soup cups and placed them in a pan of warm sudsy water. "As a matter of fact, I baked extra for you to take home."

A few minutes later, everyone sat around the table and joined hands. Bea was certain a bolt of lightning had struck her when Tate wrapped his calloused hand around hers. She tried to concentrate on the prayer Clive was giving. Her mind refused to cooperate. The thought of leaving Tate and Holly was becoming more and more painful. In less than four days, they had become a necessary part of her life. She couldn't imagine having to face a day without them. She had no right to such fanciful thoughts.

"Amen and dig in," Clive concluded the prayer.

"Dr. Bea?" Martha bumped her arm, a bowl of boiled potatoes in her hand.

Bea's mind was a blizzard of sensations. "Sorry, I guess I was daydreaming."

Martha grinned. "I reckon I know why." She laughed outright and winked at her husband. "Where's the mistletoe when you need it?"

Bea gasped, too petrified to look at Tate. She grabbed the dish of boiled potatoes and plopped two on her plate while searching for a way to change the subject. *Kissing.*

When she scooped a potato onto Holly's plate, the little girl said, "Why is your face so red, Dr. Bea?" She brightened. "If you get p'monia, me and Daddy will take care of you, and that means you'd have to stay longer."

Tate raised his eyebrows at Bea, locking her gaze with his. "I think if a little girl doesn't clean her plate, she might be sent to bed without enjoying a slice of Miz Martha's pumpkin pie."

Bea thought he looked a little weary when he reached over to tussle his daughter's hair. Thankfully, Martha changed the subject. "Clive drove me into town day before yesterday. A fierce wind had blown right down the center of Main Street. Sent ornaments and Christmas bows skittering down the street like tumbleweeds. Even blew the mercantile sign right off'n its hooks."

"Yep," Clive interrupted, "the wind was so strong it took all I could do to get Martha and me inside the store."

Bea was thankful for the conversation that drew attention away from a nonexistent relationship between her and Tate. While she and Holly cleared the table, Martha rewarded each of them with a generous slice of pumpkin pie topped with sweetened clotted cream.

Martha's cheeks pinked at all the praises. She twittered, "Land's sake, I don't know when I've ever had so many compliments. Makes a soul feel plumb appreciated."

The clock on the mantel chimed three.

It was all beyond Bea's belief that the day had flown past when the Jimsons announced they needed to take their leave before it was too dark to travel. She had packed her meager belongings while Holly and Tate napped. Although her heart told her differently, common sense told her it was time to return to town.

She remembered Tate's kiss and hesitated a moment before announcing that it was time for her to also depart. A loud pounding on the door and a frantic male voice saved her from having to say a heart-wrenching goodbye.

Clive opened the door. The appearance of Ian Murphy took them all by surprise. Bea rushed to Olive and Shamus Murphy's son and drew him inside. "Is there an emergency in town?"

The boy spoke through chattering teeth. He briefly relayed about the wind storm that had blown through town. "My pa was on the ladder trying to re-hang the store's sign. I was in the storeroom reading a book about the famous outlaw Jesse James. I should've been out there holding the ladder."

Martha shoved a cup of coffee into his hand. "Here, this'll warm you up."

He shook his head. "There's no time. Thank you just the same, Miz Jimson." He cast a fretful look toward Bea. "He's hurt bad, Dr. Bea. You gotta come now."

Clive said, "Boy, you best swallow down that hot coffee. It's a long, cold ride back to town."

Tate spoke up. "His horse is probably worn out from plowing ten miles through belly-deep snow, and Dr. Bea's horse is old and slow. It'll be after dark before she gets to town. Clive, if you don't mind, would you hitch my gelding to her buggy?"

Ian swallowed down the coffee and set the cup on the table. "My horse'll be fine. I'll just be getting on to let Ma know Dr. Bea is on her way."

Tate snapped, "No, you won't. You'll not leave her to travel alone." He added, "You will leave your horse here and ride in the buggy with her."

Clive hefted into his jacket. Martha handed him his winter hat. He pulled the flaps down over his ears and crooked his finger at Ian. "Boy, you run to the barn and get Tate's gelding and hitch him to my buggy while I unhitch one of my Belgians. Randy is strong enough to pull a barn half way 'cross the county. He's strong and likes to work. He'll get you and Dr. Bea to town without working up a good sweat."

Bea had grabbed her medical satchel and brown leather traveling bag. She dared a look at Tate. His glassy eyes worried her. It meant he was still feverish. He managed a weak smile that turned to a grimace as a coughing spell overtook him.

He met her concerned gaze with a bleary-eyed defiance. "Just give me a shot of tonic, and I'll be fine."

She removed a pair of woolen socks from her travel bag and pulled them over her feet. Holly held out Bea's traveling boots. While Bea laced them up, she explained to Martha, "Heat a kettle of water. Then cover his head and shoulders with a towel. Holly, do you think you can hold the towel over your father's head so that it forms a tent?"

The little girl nodded. Bea said, "Good." She turned to Martha. "While Tate is bent over the basin, slowly fill it with steaming water."

She reached inside her medical satchel and removed a large jar. She asked Holly to get a clean cup. Bea filled half the cup with camphor crystals. She instructed Martha to add a tablespoon of camphor to the steaming water.

She looked at Tate. "Breathe. Inhale the steam. It will help clear your lungs." She also instructed Martha to give him a tablespoon of tonic every few hours. "If you could sit with him for the night, Holly and I would be grateful."

Martha said, "There's plenty of food left. Clive and

I will stay long as we're needed. You just get to town safely."

Bea helped Tate to the bedroom, where he collapsed onto the mattress. Holly and Martha hovered over him. Even though Bea didn't want to leave him, she had a duty to help an injured patient. "As soon as I tend to Mr. Murphy, and if his injury isn't serious, I'll return to check on you."

Tate reached out and grabbed her hand. "I hope the people of Landry have the good sense to know what a treasure they've got, having you as their doctor."

Clive called out, "Dr. Bea? Got the buggy hitched up. I'll put your bags in it."

Holly clasped her around the waist. "I wish you didn't have to go."

Martha came to the rescue. She eased the child away. "You know, I haven't tasted any of Dr. Bea's cookies. What did you call them?"

A tearful Holly said, "Krispy Kringles."

"That's right. Why don't you set some out on a plate?"

"No, I don't want to."

"Holly…" Bea knelt and lifted the child's chin. "I'm a doctor. I swore an oath to take care of the sick and the injured. You knew when I came to take care of your father that I'd be leaving as soon as he was better. You're old enough to understand that I have a responsibility. Besides, you have Princess to keep you company, and you can read *Black Beauty* to your father while he rests."

The child sighed. "Okay."

Bea's heart crumbled like one of her cookies when she hugged the child. At the door, she looked over

Holly's shoulder. Tate rewarded her with a nod and a weak smile. "Merry Christmas, Dr. Bea, and thank you."

Chapter Eleven

Cold air nipped her flesh. Bea shivered, thankful for her heavy coat and for the meager heat generated by the lad sitting next to her. Snow swirled with a blinding force.

True to Clive's testament, the muscular Belgian gelding trotted through the snow with little effort. The boy next to her sat silent, huddled under the quilt. She prompted, "Tell me about your father's injury."

He cast her a beleaguered look. "Ma got some men to carry him to your office. All I know is he was in a lot of pain, and there was blood dribbling from his mouth."

Bleeding from the mouth was not good. Bea knew this signaled a possible internal injury. Even with her skill as a surgeon she did not have the necessary facility or equipment to treat this type of wound.

When she didn't comment, the boy said, "If he dies, it'll be my fault. I heard Mrs. Talbot tell her daughter to stay away from me because I was a lazy good-for-nothing. At first, what she said made me mad, but she's right. I am lazy. My parents never require anything of me, so I just don't do anything."

"Jeannie is a pretty girl. Do you like her?"

Bea felt his sigh. "Yeah, as a friend." He looked at Bea. "Can I tell you something in confidence?"

She nodded. "Of course."

He hesitated. His voice sounded raw and hollow. "I

don't want to be a storekeeper. I want to go to England and study journalism. I want to travel the world and see all the things I've read about in books, and then become a famous writer like Ned Buntline or Prentiss Ingraham. My parents can't know. They'd be more disappointed in me than they are already."

She heard him take in a breath. "Ian, you have wonderfully understanding parents. Once I tend to your father and see that his condition is stable, I'll sit with you while you talk to your mother. I'm certain you'll find her supportive of your dream."

Before they could continue their conversation, the chestnut gelding snorted and tugged against the reins. Silhouettes of the outskirts of town rose through the gray. Bea loosened the long leathers a bit, allowing the Belgian to gallop. "I believe Randy is as ready to get out of the cold as we are."

She guided the horse down the hill to Main Street, halting in front of her office. When Ian made to exit the buggy to assist her down, she said, "I'll just grab my bags. You take the horse to the livery. Be sure Mr. Hofstetter gives Randy an extra scoop of oats and puts a warming blanket on him."

She alit from the buggy and hastened to its rear to grab her baggage from the buggy's boot. She called out, "Go!"

Ian clucked the Belgian into action. "Tell Ma I'll be in soon as I take care of the horse."

Christmas Day and the town looked dark and deserted. Bea's weather-worn office shingle hung lopsided from a single chain. It squeaked in protest as the wind rocked it back and forth. She shook her head at the broken sign, then hiked her skirt to step on the boardwalk and to the door of her home and medical office. The moment she stepped inside, she began shedding her heavy garments. "Olive, I'm here."

Olive Murphy stepped from behind the curtain that separated the waiting area from the examination room. She held out her hands. "Oh, thank God you're here. I was afraid the weather might keep you from traveling."

Bea shucked out of her gloves and tossed them aside. She grabbed a fresh apron from a cabinet and donned it while she stepped to where the supine, ashen Shamus Murphy lay. "Tell me what you know about his condition."

Olive said, "He has a broken leg. It's the blood from his mouth that worries me."

Bea pulled back the sheet. "When did this happen?"

"This morning. I've given him laudanum to keep him quiet and to ease his pain."

Bea nodded. "That's good. Grab a pair of scissors and cut off the pants, then remove his shirt while I wash my hands. I'll need to exam him to determine the extent of internal injuries before setting his leg."

Bea rolled up her long dress sleeves. She poured steaming water into a basin and grabbed a bar of lye soap, scrubbed her arms and hands, and dried them with a clean towel. She bent over Shamus Murphy, nude except for the sheet covering his lower extremities.

She pointed out the large purple bruise next to his ribcage. After gently probing the area, Bea straightened.

"It's bad, isn't it?" A worried frown furrowed Olive's brow.

Bea spoke in a lowered tone. "Bad enough. A fractured rib. He'll have difficulty breathing, and he'll be in pain for several weeks."

"What about the bleeding…is it internal?"

"Fortunately, the rib isn't broken, which means no punctured lung. There must be another reason for the blood."

Although his breathing was shallow, Bea attributed that to the laudanum and not a punctured lung. She opened his mouth. "Hold the lantern where I can see inside."

Olive obeyed.

Bea heaved a relieved sigh. "No wonder there was blood." She pointed to the inside of Shamus' mouth. "He's near bitten through his tongue. Thankfully it doesn't require stitches, although he'll have problems eating for a while."

A voice called out, "Ma? Dr. Bea?"

Olive answered, "In here, son."

"Good. I'm glad you're here, Ian." Bea eyed the scrawny lad. "I need to set your father's broken leg. Even in his unconscious state the pain may cause him to flinch. We certainly don't want him falling off the table. Are you strong enough to pin his shoulders down to hold him steady?"

Olive stepped next to her son and said, "We'll both hold him. Do what is necessary, Bea."

****

Bea didn't realize how weary she was until after she settled in a chair with a cup of hot tea in her hands. She smiled at her friend and then at the boy. "Olive, Ian has something important to tell you. I hope you will listen with an open mind."

Olive raised her brows. "I'm not sure I can take anymore upsets today."

Ian set his cup aside and stood. He paced around the

room, then sat. He cleared his throat. The tips of his ears glowed red. He glanced at Bea, who nodded encouragement. He inhaled and exhaled. "Okay, Ma…Mother, I wish Pa could hear me so I don't have to tell this but once. The truth is, as much as I love you and Pa…umm…Father, I don't want to be a storekeeper, and I don't want to spend the rest of my life in Landry." He went on to recount his true desires.

Silence filled the room. As much as she desired to intervene, Bea forced herself to remain quiet.

Olive ran a finger around the cup's rim. She fiddled with the napkin in her lap. Tears welled in her eyes. "I have a confession to make. One day when I was cleaning your room, I found a stack of stories you had written. I wasn't snooping. They were on your desk, and I accidentally knocked them off when I was dusting. Ian, you have a wonderful way with words. You have a talent that shouldn't be wasted."

She stood and cupped her son's face between her hands. "I, too, have longed to see the world. I married, instead. Oh, don't get me wrong. I do love your father very much." She returned to her seat. "I have a little of my own money set aside. I don't know how far it will take you, but it's yours, nonetheless."

Ian looked at his mother with an appreciative smile. "I'm not sure Father will approve."

As was her habit, Olive clasped her hands together and held them under her chin. "Don't fret about your father. I know how to placate him. For now, I'll need you to help with running the store."

Bea noticed that the Ian's lips had quirked into a smile. She said, "I'll leave the two of you to sit with Shamus while I indulge myself in a nice hot bath."

Olive remarked, "How rude of me. I've not thought to ask about Tate Reed."

Bea's eyes widened with pleasure. "Let's just say that I've had an unusual Christmas. I'll tell you all about it—after I've had my bath."

Chapter Twelve

Tate could hardly believe a fever would drain so much of his strength in twenty-four hours. "I seem to have slept away the day," he said as Martha collected the tray of empty dishes.

"You've slept away two whole days. At least your appetite has returned. That's a good sign that you're well enough for Clive to take me home."

"I'm mighty grateful to you for looking after Holly and nursing me back to health."

"Pshaw, I can't take all the credit. It was mostly Dr. Bea and her med'cine. I don't know what them little white pills are that she left for me to give you. A miracle cure, if'n you ask me, which you ain't."

She stood holding the tray, and wearing an undecided expression. Tate wasn't sure if he wanted to ask what was on her mind. "I can see you have more to say, Martha. Has Holly misbehaved?"

The elderly woman harrumphed. "Land sakes, that sweet child has cried her eyes out since Dr. Bea left. That little girl needs a mama. I swear, and I never swear, but Tate Reed, sick or not, you don't have the brains God gave a gopher. Even a blind man could see how you looked at Dr. Bea."

Tate held up his hand. "Whoa, stop. What are you talking about?"

"Love at first sight, you ninny. I don't know what

Bea put in them cookies, but I can tell you that ever since Clive and me have eaten them…" Her face flushed red, and she almost tripped over her tongue when she said, "Never you mind 'bout that. The truth is, you and Bea have strong feelings for each other. Now what're you gonna do 'bout it? Put that in your pipe and smoke it."

Martha traipsed out of the bedroom without looking over her shoulder. He called, "Where's Holly?"

"In the barn collectin' eggs."

Tate wobbled when he swung his legs over the edge of the bed and stood. He needed to get dressed and move around. He stared out the window. Martha's words rolled around inside his head. He turned away from the window and paced around the room. The notion of remarrying had never really entered his mind. After Mary's death, he'd had no desire to see other women.

Had he truly gotten over her death? He didn't know. Yet the idea Martha had planted in his mind wouldn't go away. Its hold seemed to grow with each ticking of the clock. He couldn't blame Martha. She may have been the first to put the thought into words, but she was right, he was strongly attracted to the beautiful doctor. He enjoyed her company, and the nearness of her had aroused him in a way that Mary never had.

Mary is dead. Bea is alive.

He stood again at the window. It seemed it was the first time in two years he'd noticed the beauty of the land—snow-laden tree limbs, a white ribbon of snow adorning the fences, a tiny snow mountain on the top of each fence post. He turned away. Everything about the last few days, especially Christmas, seemed unreal, like a dream distorting his sense of reality.

He hadn't heard the door open. "Daddy?"

"Come in, Holly."

"There's only two Krispy Kringles left. Miz Martha said I should share." She held out the round cookie covered in powdered sugar that reminded him of snow.

Holly sat on the edge of his bed. She finished off her cookie in two bites. "Do you think Dr. Bea will come back?"

"It's too cold, and the snow is too deep for her to travel such a long way."

The little girl hung her head. "I wish she was my mommy."

He didn't dare admit that he wished the same thing. His mind told him it wasn't possible. His heart said otherwise.

He plopped the sugary goodness of his cookie into his mouth and chewed. In doing so, something inside him changed. The life he'd had with Mary in West Virginia and then in Cheyenne was in the past. With sudden unmistakable clarity he was ready to let go of the past and build a new life, and with only one woman.

He didn't know how this quiet, unassuming woman had invaded his life and performed a miracle. He wanted to tell her how much she meant to him. How much he loved her.

Mary had often berated him for never saying *I love you*. Now that he thought about it, he had never loved her—not truly. He'd been in love with the idea that a woman of her social standing and unmatched beauty would give him a second glance, let alone marry him. It stung to finally admit to himself that she had only wed him to make her ex-beau jealous.

He sat on the edge of the bed. As soon as the weather cleared enough for him to ride to town, he planned to tell

Dr. Beata Inseldorf that he loved her, and he would never stop telling her.

****

Once Shamus was settled in the Murphys' living quarters above the mercantile, Bea wearily climbed the stairs to her own apartment and retired for the evening. Relishing the comfort of her goose-down mattress, she forgot how uncomfortable it was to sit up all night in a hard-slatted rocking chair. Bea closed her eyes, but she remained restless. She lay in a tight ball, waiting for her body to warm beneath her flannel nightgown and the double layer of quilts.

It was some time before she drifted off to sleep, and when she did, Tate Reed appeared in her dreams. He kissed her. A warm feeling spread through her entire body. She accepted the invitation when he opened his arms to bring her more fully against the contour of his muscular physique. He murmured *I love you* against her lips. Hands down, this was what she wanted. It made her feel desirable and contented. It made her feel almost like a married woman with a husband and a child to care for. His kissed her neck and explored her in regions that no man had ever touched.

Heat roared through her body. Her breath came in short bursts, and her belly twisted in a delicious responsiveness. Her eyes flew open. Confusion followed as she tossed back the quilts and swung her legs over the side of the bed. The flannel nightgown's warmth stifled her. Perspiration collected between her breasts.

The cold floor on the bottoms of her bare feet helped cool the hotness that seared through her. It was a dream, she chided. A dream filled with an urgent sensation she had never experienced.

Sensual desire!

This presented a problem. She had no idea what to do with it.

Chapter Thirteen

Lonely. That's how he felt. A week had passed, and Tate tried not to think of Bea and the brief kiss they had shared. He spoke to the image in the mirror. "If only I could forget the way her blue eyes crinkled when she smiled, or the taste of her sweet lips."

A knock sounded at the door, interrupting his thoughts. "Daddy?"

"Come in, Holly."

His daughter stood with her hands behind her back. A mischievous grin twinkled in her eyes. Tate lifted his eyebrows. Curious, he said, "Are you hiding something?"

Holly rocked back on her heels. Tate thought she looked as if she were pondering how to answer his question. "Holly?"

She lifted her gaze to him. "Miz Martha said it was tr'dition to kiss somebody when they stood under the mistletoe." She held forth a clump of green leaves filled with white and red berries. "I was thinking that maybe you could go to town and hold the mistletoe over Dr. Bea's head." She hastened on without drawing a breath. "And then you could kiss her and ask her to marry us, and she would say yes, and then she could be my mommy."

He knelt on one knee and removed the mistletoe from her little hand. The sincerity in his daughter's eyes gripped Tate's heart. He touched her cheek. "It's a little late. Christmas is over."

"You ninny." Martha stood at the bedroom's doorway. "I come to tell you about the New Year's Eve dance tomorrow night. Even the young'uns can attend."

When it looked as if Tate might object, the old woman prattled on. "Me and Clive are going." She smiled down at the little girl. "Wear your prettiest dress and get your daddy to fix up your hair." She squinted a frown at Tate. "And you wear your best glad-rags and dab on some of that smell-goody aftershave lotion. We'll pick you and Holly up 'bout three."

Clive entered the room and grinned over his wife's shoulder. "Bossy, ain't she?" He held a sprig of mistletoe over Martha's head.

She twittered like a young schoolgirl when her husband pecked her on the cheek. "Anyhow," she said to Holly, "pack a nighty, 'cause after midnight is too late to drive back to the ranch. We're staying at the boardin' house." She looked at Tate. "We booked a room for you, too, and we'll tend to Holly"—she cleared her throat—"if you decide to use the mistletoe to help with a little sparkin'."

Chapter Fourteen

She stood behind the long buffet table, engrossed in conversation with Olive Murphy. Tate took in the gentle movements of Bea's slender hands as she lifted Krispy Kringles from a box to a platter. He thought she looked more beautiful than anyone had a right to look. The red satin gown enhanced her creamy complexion, and her hair pulled up on one side with luxurious curls draped over her shoulder reminded him of rays of sunshine. He moved across the floor to where she stood.

Holly let go of her father's hand and skipped across the room. "Dr. Bea?"

His heart practically turned over when Bea smiled at his daughter and then at him. He touched his coat where a sprig of mistletoe tied with a red bow nestled in his pocket. He didn't quite remember walking to the table and reaching for one of Bea's magical cookies or popping it into his mouth.

She came around the table and brushed sugar from the front of his brown tweed jacket. He thought her voice sounded like silk when she said, "I was hoping you would come."

"You were?"

"Uh-huh."

The band leader called out, "Gents, grab your favorite gal. Our first dance is a waltz."

Tate held out his hand. Pressing gently against her

back, he glided her around the room. When he held her in his arms, he knew it wasn't intrigue or lust that he felt for Bea. It was something far stronger and more powerful.

When the waltz ended, Bea gave him an uncertain look. "My goodness, the barn seems to have grown awfully hot and stuffy."

Before he could respond, the band struck up a lively reel, and Bea was swept away from him. The evening passed in a blur, and not once did Tate get the opportunity to hold Bea in his arms again.

He passed the evening sharing dances with his daughter, Martha, and a few other ladies. He often found himself on the sidelines or at the food table sampling the feast of goodies. Holly tugged on his sleeve. "Daddy, you have to make a wish."

He cast his daughter a curious glance. "A wish for what?"

"Miz Martha says you have to make a wish for something you're gonna do in the New Year."

Tate laughed. "I believe Miz Martha meant to say that it's tradition to make a resolution for things you're going to work on or wish will happen in the New Year."

Holly grabbed the last two Krispy Kringles. She held one out to her father. "Oh, then my New Year's res'lution is to wish that you would ask Dr. Bea to marry you."

He scooped the precocious eight-year-old into his arms and enjoyed the cookie as he waltzed her across the room. "Holly, this is the last time we're gonna have this conversation. A man and a woman need to get to know each other before they consider marriage. They can't just up and get married."

71

She cupped Tate's face with her tiny hands. "But why can't they?"

He sighed. How did he explain that he was out of the doctor's social league and that as a handyman he couldn't financially support a family? Instead, he said, "If the man and woman discovered they didn't like each other, then they might decide to go their separate ways. That would hurt everyone involved." He tweaked his daughter's nose. "And that includes a little girl with a big heart. Understand?"

Holly yawned. She laid her head on his shoulder. "I guess."

It was plain that his daughter was tuckered out. He crossed the floor to where his friends waited. Clive held out his arms to take the little girl in his arms, but Tate continued to hold her. "Martha and I are callin' it a night. We ain't spring chickens no more, and all this dancin' has got our ol' bones squawkin' for bed. We can take Holly along and get her tucked in while you do some more dancin' with that pretty doctor."

Tate offered an understanding nod. He glanced around the room and spotted Bea in what appeared to be deep conversation with Aaron Mindel, the banker, an eligible bachelor. "I think I'll call it a night, too."

Martha cuffed Tate on the arm. "She's not interested in that foppish dandy. I have it on good word that she's plannin' to buy the empty dress shop next to her office and convert it into a hospital. Dr. Bea and he are more'n likely talking business." She gave Tate her special look. The one that expressed, *You better do what I say or else.* "Don't worry about Holly. I'll put 'er to bed and stay until you return." She ruffled herself like an irritated hen. "If'n you've got the brains that God gave a gopher, then you'll get on over there and stick close so when the clock strikes midnight you can grab Dr. Bea and kiss her. And I don't mean a peck on the cheek. I'm talkin' 'bout planting a real smack-a-roo on her lips, and then escort her home."

Clive cut in. "Son, Martha and me been married nigh on fifty years, and I can tell you that a woman can't read your mind. You gotta tell her how you feel."

Aggravation hung in Tate's craw. He knew his friends meant well. However, his business was none of theirs. "Clive…Martha, I appreciate your concern about my love life." He shifted his sleeping daughter in his arms. "Here's the thing…I'm a handyman with nothing to offer a sophisticated, professional woman like Bea Inseldorf. It's nothing against the two of you, because I'm grateful for my job and the roof over my head."

Martha skewered him with a mean eye. She harrumphed. "Bea's Pap was a goat farmer. He made cheese and sold goat's milk, and traipsed around in bib overalls and rubber boots, 'cept on Sunday when he'd dress for church. Her Ma was a doctor. The rest is history."

Clive's eyes narrowed. "C'mon, Martha. You're just whistlin' in the wind." To Tate, he said, "Stay or go. 'S'up to you. We'll be headin' back to the ranch after breakfast."

Tate relinquished his daughter to Clive's open arms. He helped Martha adjust the woolen cloak over her shoulders.

****

Bea ended her conversation with the banker by shaking his hand and saying she would see him on Tuesday to sign the necessary loan papers.

Her breath caught in her throat when she spotted Tate helping Martha with her cloak. A searing sadness shot through her. He was leaving. Had he purposely avoided her after their first and only dance? She debated on whether to join the small group before they departed or pretend she didn't know they had left the festivities.

She had known Tate for such a short time, but his gentle spirit and obvious love for his child had captured her heart. She decided to join the small knot to wish them a Happy New Year. Her heart thudded as she approached the Jimsons and Tate.

She pasted on an overly bright smile to hide her nervousness. "Leaving so soon?"

She wondered at the odd look Martha cast Tate. Martha said, "We've had enough partying to last 'til the next time. We told Tate we'd tend to Holly so he could stay 'til midnight and ring in the New Year."

Bea smiled up at the handsome man standing next to her. "That's a delightful idea. It's fun celebrating with a group of wonderful friends, but not so much without a special someone." She hoped Tate picked up on the cue.

Her heart practically turned over when his sultry brown eyes twinkled and his mouth curved upward. He thanked Clive and Martha for watching after his daughter. He offered his arm to Bea. "Shall we get a cup of punch?"

Several gents came by asking for a dance. To each of them Bea offered a gracious smile and said, "I'm sorry, but my dance card is filled for the rest of the evening."

****

Someone dimmed the lanterns, giving the room a romantic ambiance as the band softly played "The Blue

Danube." Tate placed Bea's hand in his and drew her close. She gazed up at him, and he savored the warm soft curves of her body.

The band leader called out, "'Tis almost midnight, folks. If you haven't already, grab your special gal, and let's start the countdown."

As soon as the count ended on one, the town clock chimed twelve times. Tate opened Bea's palm and dropped a kiss on it. She stared at him for a heart-stopping moment before he lowered his mouth to hers. His lips brushed hers tenderly, awakening feelings within him that were bold and exciting.

When she offered no resistance, he tightened his strong arms around her waist and pulled her closer. His heart thumped against his chest when she gazed at him with heated eyes. It beat even harder when his mouth swooped down to recapture her lips, this time with more intensity. Never had he felt more virile or needed than he did at this moment.

Working her arms around his neck, she melted against him and returned his kiss with equal ardor. Lost in the moment, he was shocked when she suddenly pulled away.

"I'm sorry," she stammered. "You must think I'm a wanton woman. I never should have…"

An awkward silence followed, and she drew in a breath. His lips burned with the memory of her kiss. He discounted her protests with a wave of his hand. He tilted his head, not sure what to say. He arched an eyebrow. "I think I might need your services as a doctor."

She gasped and awarded him with an incredulous stare. He hastened on. "You see, Holly believes there's magic in the cookies you bake. She believes if I eat enough of them, her wish for me to ask you to marry me would come true."

He cupped his hands around Bea's face. "The truth is, I've eaten so many of those danged Krispy Kringles that I've got a stomach ache, or maybe I've got a stomach ache because I've fallen in love with you and feel like a foolish schoolboy holding you in my arms. Krispy Kringles or not, Bea, I'm not a man of means, and I don't begin to pretend that I'd fit into your world. All I know is that Holly had the best Christmas ever."

Bea tiptoed and pressed her lips to his—a whisper of a kiss. "What about you?"

She was way too beautiful, especially when she smiled. Maybe it was the season, because he wasn't usually that open about his feelings. "Best ever for me, too."

Amid all the cheering of Happy New Year and the noisemakers and the singing of "Auld Lang Syne," Bea regarded him intently. "How about a warm fire and a glass of wine?"

Chapter Fifteen

To avoid any town gossip, Bea led Tate up the back stairs to her small apartment. She offered him the one comfortable chair while she poured elderberry wine into two fluted goblets. She held one out and said, "I'm well aware there's a guarded side to you. Because of your past experience with love, you've become cautious." She rewarded him with a kind smile. "You don't need to be wary of me."

He remembered the story she'd told him about the differences between her mother and father, and then tonight Martha had reminded him again. He regarded Bea intently. The expression on her face changed as she adjusted her skirts to sit in a cane-back chair. His heart dropped to the pit of his stomach. He'd let a prime opportunity slip past by waiting too long to respond. Martha was right—he didn't have the brains God gave a gopher. Not when it came to Bea Inseldorf.

"Tate, there are things you should know about me. And please, just listen." His heart tripped over itself when she ran the pink tip of her tongue around her lips to catch a droplet of wine. He listened as she began, "I am twenty-eight years old. By today's standards, that makes me an old maid and possibly too old to bear children. Maybe the reason I've never married is because I'm not a conformist. I've met handsome men that I've never given a second glance because they aren't my type.

I don't like men who are shallow, and I do not tolerate arrogance. I'd rather enjoy a buggy ride in the country and a picnic by a stream than getting all dressed up and attending parties."

Her voice grew more emphatic. "I can fix a leaky faucet, milk goats, wade around ankle deep in goat poop, deliver babies, tend gunshot wounds, and I don't faint at the sight of blood. What I'm trying to say is that I'm not very feminine, and if that's what you're looking for, then…you'd better count me out and move on with your life."

She huffed out a breath. "I hate to disabuse you of the notion that all I desire is hobnobbing with the elite. But what I really prefer are quiet evenings after a long day of tending ailing folks and patching up injured cowboys."

Tate lifted his eyes in mock alarm. He reached out and clasped both her hands, pulling her into his lap. He nuzzled her ear and inhaled the subtle sweetness of her rose water. He said, "I can read and write and I'm fairly decent at arithmetic, so all this philosophical discussion aside, I think you're absolutely perfect."

He sought to find a more suitable description. "To me, you are like a…warm breeze on a sunny afternoon and a…mixture of sweet mysticism like your Krispy Kringle cookies."

Bea's laughter was warm and infectious, and he couldn't help but think that this was how life was supposed to be—the joy of another person's presence, and definitely the magic of their laughter.

Epilogue

Christmas Eve, 1881

Bea sat at the kitchen table. With her family sleeping upstairs, the house was quiet as she dipped the pen into the ink pot. She wrote, *It has been a whirlwind year— marriage to the most wonderful man, and gaining a delightful, loving daughter at the same time. In September, we celebrated the grand opening of Landry General Hospital. I had the good fortune to acquire the services of Dr. Eamon Wise, a skilled surgeon, and his wife, Amelia, an equally skilled nurse.*

Tate and I moved into my childhood home on Beaker Street. He used his carpenter skills to expand my old upstairs apartment to add a bedroom, and a water closet complete with a new pull-chain toilet, for the comfort of Dr. and Mrs. Wise.

Clive and Martha have, more or less, become Holly's adoptive grandparents. Much to our surprise, Clive drew up a new will leaving the Rockin' J to Tate, stating that he had become like a son to them.

She stopped to sniff the delectable spicy aroma filling her kitchen. She smiled as she moved to the stove and opened the oven door to remove two trays of little round balls. Holly had helped crush sugar granules into powdery sweetness. Tomorrow morning, the little girl would roll the cookies to coat them. Bea sat once again and lifted the pen. She smiled as she smoothed her hand over the tiny mound hidden beneath her apron. *Tomorrow is Christmas, and what more fitting day to share my exciting news.*

****

Christmas afternoon

The dishes were washed, leftover food sat in the icebox, and the kitchen sparkled clean. The Christmas gifts had been opened and torn wrapping paper no longer littered the living room floor. The clock above the mantel chimed six, and a knock sounded at the front door. Bea asked Holly to invite their guests to the parlor.

Tate strolled into the kitchen. He bent to nuzzle Bea's neck. "Merry Christmas. Happy?"

She balanced the tray of spiced cookies, and purred. "More than happy."

He grabbed the carafe of warm cider and followed his wife to the parlor to greet Clive and Martha, Olive and Shamus, Eamon and Amelia. The room filled with delightful squeals when Clive held out a black puppy to Holly. The old man said, "You gotta give him a strong name."

Holly held the wiggly black bundle to her chest. She hugged Clive. It seemed the room waited for the girl to name the little dog. Finally she said, "Henry."

"Henry! Well, I don't—" Martha jabbed her husband in the ribs. He coughed. "I think Henry is a fine name."

The room filled with laughter and good-natured chatter as Bea passed around a silver salver of cookies. She deposited the tray on the sideboard and went to stand next to the chair where her husband sat. She cleared her throat. "Everyone, may I have your attention for a moment?"

Tate looked up at her, his eyes filled with concern. Bea leaned to feather a kiss on his lips. She smiled as she lovingly smoothed her hand over the little bump. "Holly, what is the seventh month of the New Year?"

The child gave her stepmother a puzzled look. She said the months out loud. "July is the seventh month. Why?"

Bea's face almost hurt from the wide grin and the words bubbled out with joy. "Because that's when you will have a baby brother or a baby sister."

She feared Tate might break her ribs if he squeezed her any tighter. When all the laughter and congratulations and slaps on the back had settled down, Tate grabbed a cookie off the tray and lifted his cup of cider. "Here's to another Krispy Kringle Christmas. There really is magic in these little balls of sweetness."

He flashed his wife a rascally gleam. Bea gave him a wicked look in return as she followed his gaze up the stairs to where she knew that after the house was quiet, they'd enjoy a night of pleasure in their oversized bed.

Tate's warm, rich laughter filled Bea. He was her future, her destiny, and her one true love for all time.

Gingerbread Knight

by

Pam Binder

Christmas Cookies

Dedication

To my lovely sister, Marilyn
who loves cookies as much as I do.

Chapter One

"Keep the cookbook safe," the old woman said. "But don't open it."

Devon Avery studied the field-green cookbook with the gold clasp that the shopkeeper had given her. She hadn't been interested in the moldy old thing before. But now that she'd been told not to open it, all she could think about was how to break the clasp.

She hated the word "no," and all the words and phrases like "can't," and "shouldn't," and "you'd better not." Each one acted like a call to arms to do the exact opposite. Not that it had helped. No matter how she tried, and wished it were different, she was an abysmal failure when it came to magic and casting spells. She should make peace with it, her mother said, but it wasn't easy. She felt as though she were letting her family down.

But that was all beside the point. Her focus was on finding her grandmother, who of late was always wandering off. Devon was worried about her grandmother, not just today but over the last few months. Her behavior had become more and more erratic, and this morning she'd walked out without letting anyone know where she was going. Devon's family was catering a Renaissance-themed wedding on a nearby estate in Stratford, England, the believed birthplace of William Shakespeare, when her grandmother left. Her mother blamed the onslaught of some sort of dementia, but

Devon didn't want to believe that was the issue and had volunteered to find her grandmother. So far, all efforts had failed.

Reluctantly, Devon handed the cookbook back to the woman. "Thank you, but I'm not interested in another cookbook. I have plenty. Especially one that you say I mustn't open."

Devon had been searching for her grandmother, and the musty bookstore seemed the logical place to start. It was exactly the kind of place her grandmother loved. The store was a blend of used books and all things magical from crystals to jewelry made from semi-precious stones. The icing on the cake was the shopkeeper. She had that wise-woman vibe, with chin-length white-blonde hair, hoop earrings, rings on all her fingers, and stacks of bead bracelets on each wrist. In a lot of ways she reminded Devon of her grandmother.

"As I mentioned when I first came in, I'm looking for my grandmother. She's about five feet tall, wears her white hair about the length of yours, and her eyes are the same color as mine—one green and one blue. Oh, and like me, she's dressed in clothes like those worn by servants in the time of Queen Elizabeth I." Devon paused. "My family is catering the wedding on the Dundee estate this weekend. You may have heard the legend, that the Dundee's ancestors hosted Queen Elizabeth I and her court over the Twelve Days of Christmas celebration, although there isn't a record of it in the history books."

"Most legends contain a pinch of truth." The shopkeeper pushed the cookbook back into Devon's hands and smiled. "You have your grandmother's eyes, one blue and one green. I understand now why Madeline wanted us to meet. She phoned, and it was her wish that I give this cookbook to you. It is a first edition from the fifteenth and sixteenth century."

Devon nodded out of politeness. The age of the cookbook explained its oldie-moldy smell, but not the shopkeeper's odd behavior or how she knew her grandmother's first name. Her grandmother never gave it out, except to family and friends. She preferred people address her as Lady Avery. "But how did my grandmother know I'd be here? And how long ago did she phone?"

"She said she'd meet you back at the estate. Shouldn't you be getting back to the estate's kitchen before your gingerbread cookies burn?"

Relief washed over her. Her grandmother was safe. The shopkeeper's warning about the gingerbread cookies burning was odd, to say the least. She'd made the cookies and put them in the oven before she left, but she hadn't turned on the oven. The cookies only took ten minutes to bake, and she had sensed it would take a while to find her grandmother. But then, Devon had grown up with odd, strange, and weird. All the women in her family had magical abilities except Devon. They had said she'd come into her magic when she turned twenty-one. That had been five years ago, and she was still waiting.

"How did you know I was baking gingerbread?" Devon lowered her voice even though they were alone in the store. "Do you have magical abilities?"

Instead of answering Devon, the shopkeeper shoved Devon out of the store like she was shooing a swarm of misbehaving school children. Once Devon had crossed the threshold, the woman shut the glass door, rattling the door chimes.

Devon turned the door handle, but it was already locked. She waved to get the shopkeeper's attention and held up the cookbook. "I don't want this."

The shopkeeper turned over the sign to read Closed, then flipped off the lights and disappeared into the store.

"Just peachy." She'd return the cookbook later. Devon stuffed the cookbook into a pocket in her long skirts and retraced her steps through the quaint town that reminded her of a village in a Jane Austen novel.

She and her grandmother shared a love of English history, and the opportunity to cater a Renaissance-themed event was the reason her grandmother had agreed to cater the Dundee wedding.

Her mother was the marketing and business genius and had expanded their cozy bake shop in Seattle, Washington into a global catering enterprise. The expansion came at a cost. Devon rarely saw her mother. Devon's father had died fifteen years ago of a heart attack, and as a result, her grandmother had raised her. The thought that her grandmother might be suffering from dementia broke Devon's heart.

She left the town behind and crossed the narrow bridge leading to the estate's grounds and the location of the wedding. A sudden December breeze stirred the swift river under the bridge into stiff white peaks that promised a storm. She quickened her step. Her hunt for her grandmother had taken longer than expected, and she knew her mother would be anxious. They still had a lot of prep work to do before the reception.

A long white limo honked its horn, startling Devon. She hurried to the other side of the bridge and stepped to the side to let it pass. The limo joined a procession of expensive cars and taxis transporting wedding guests toward the top of the hill and the over five-hundred-year-old estate that overlooked the town. The parents of the bride and groom had transformed the grounds of the estate to look like a Renaissance Faire, complete with booths, and with actors dressed to play the part of venders, nobles, and knights. There was even a scaled-down tournament field.

A mist rose from the river and shrouded the sun in a gossamer veil of spun silver. Threads of silver light drew her attention to the tournament field. Silhouetted against the blue-gray sky was the dark outline of a knight wearing a full set of armor and astride a black horse. She was too far away to make out his features.

One of her family's legends seeped into her thoughts—a romantic legend that had been passed down through generations of hopeful Avery women. A legend that a knight would appear to the one who possessed unlimited magical powers. As a child Devon had wished that woman would be her. When she grew older, and her magic never materialized, she'd abandoned the dream.

Then the knight turned in her direction, and in her thoughts, she heard his words. *I find lost things.*

The mist lifted, and the warning blare of a limo's horn pulled Devon's attention from the tournament field. When she looked back, the knight had vanished.

****

A new parade of vehicles filed past Devon as she reached the side entrance of the estate. She couldn't get the image of the knight and what he'd said from her thoughts. But it couldn't have been real. The logical explanation was lack of sleep, a vivid imagination, and the romantic location of the wedding. One thing was certain—she wouldn't tell her mother. Her mother would blow the incident out of proportion.

When she reached the top step leading to the kitchen's entrance, smoke billowed from an open window to greet Devon. She frowned, knowing what had happened before she opened the door. She must have turned the stove on by mistake. Drat. The smoke smelled of burnt molasses and brown sugar. Her gingerbread cookies were burning.

Inside the blindingly white kitchen, the marble counters, glossy cupboards and appliances were blanketed with smoke. She raced inside and almost tripped over her long skirts. Recovering before she slammed into the island counter, she sped over to the oven, pulled out the tray of smoking cookies, and placed it on a trivet on the counter. She could have sworn she hadn't turned on the oven before she left to find her grandmother. Her heart sank. The cookies were a charred disaster. She'd have to make a new batch.

Instead of a wedding cake the bride had requested a tier of sugar cookies, topped with the bride and groom made from gingerbread. Devon had planned to decorate the gingerbread bride in white and silver frosting that resembled tiny pearls and crystals and the gingerbread groom as a knight. It had seemed such a good idea at the time.

She opened the windows wider and waved her arms to chase out the smoke. A fire in the kitchen on the day of a wedding was a bad omen. That was the first rule an Avery learned.

"What is going on in here? You haven't burned cookies since you were six." Devon's mother entered the kitchen as regally as a queen and dressed like a noblewoman in Queen Elizabeth I's court. Her gown was butter-cream yellow, and the matching head covering hid hair she'd allowed to turn white. Her mother snapped her fingers at the ceiling alarm and instantly it turned off. "Did you find your grandmother?"

"No, but she left a message with a shopkeeper that she was headed back to the estate."

"I'm glad your grandmother is all right. Do you know why she was in town?"

"She was looking for a cookbook." Devon rolled the oversized sleeves to her elbows. Instead of a noblewoman's dress, she had chosen to wear bland, nondescript clothes which would identify her as part of the kitchen staff. Beside her mother, however, she felt like a plain peanut butter cookie next to an elaborately decorated Christmas sugar cookie. Maybe she'd change into something more festive before the wedding reception.

Her mother sighed. "Old cookbooks again. What is it with your grandmother and old recipes? As much as it pains me to say, my mother is spending more and more time in her own world and neglecting her duties in this one. She never recovered from the death of her younger sister. And as a result, and as much as it pains me to say, we need help. Would you mind if I asked your cousin Lorna to help us from time to time?"

Devon shook her head. She and Lorna had been best friends growing up, and it would be fun to have her visit. "Not at all. But Grandmother doesn't think Aunt Charlotte is dead," Devon defended. "She believes she is missing."

"I don't understand why she can't let it go. Well, what are we going to do about your gingerbread cookies?"

Her mother's quick change of topic didn't fool Devon. Her mother was as worried as Devon had been. "I'll make more."

"No time. I have a better idea." Her mother loomed over the burned cookies and snapped her fingers again. In a blink they looked baked to perfection. "There. That's better."

Devon looked longingly at the magic her mother had accomplished with a snap of her fingers. Just like turning off the fire alarm, her mother made it look effortless.

"When they're decorated," her mother was saying, "I'll ask your grandmother to animate them so they will dance on top of the cookie cake at the reception."

"Isn't that too risky?"

"We have to keep ahead of the competition. We will tell the guests that we inserted tiny batteries into the cookies and that's the reason they look like they're dancing. I had hoped you would have inherited your grandmother's magic touch in that area. My magic is limited. Maybe we are finally losing our gifts, as our magic seems to diminish with each generation. My mother keeps saying that love and magic are connected. Perhaps if you married, or at least had a boyfriend?"

"Mother, we've had this conversation before. I have a lousy track record. I've been in love and engaged and both times my heart was crushed into cookie crumbs. Grandmother suggested I try lust." The image of the knight visualized in her thoughts and her face heated. Great. She was having fantasies about men who didn't even exist except in her imagination.

"That sounds like your grandmother," her mother said as she started arranging white roses into a vase.

Devon grabbed the ugly head covering that had come with her costume and stuffed her red hair under the beige cloth. She loathed the head covering almost as much as the rules and regulations that governed her family's magic. Both made her feel penned in and confined. At least these costumes were better than the time they all had to dress like mermaids and cater a wedding held in a swimming pool. That was the worst. Someone had knocked the wedding cake into the water, and there was no way her magical mother could snap her fingers without being seen.

But that disaster aside, her family's business of themed weddings was legendary. Everyone in the industry wanted to know their secret. Her family's stock answer for their success was hard work, attention to detail, and the love of making a person's dream occasion come true. All the women in Devon's family, dating back hundreds of years, had been touched with magic. But was her mother right? Could their inherited magic finally have run its course?

They'd been so careful over the generations and adhered to the rules for casting spells. Their spells were never meant to draw attention and were what their ancestors had called household spells—spells that in some way helped make housework and cooking easier. Devon had overheard her grandmother and mother say that sometimes the men the Avery women married encouraged their wives to test the boundaries of the rules. As far as Devon knew, however, they'd not succeeded. But if she were wrong, could that be the reason the magic was deserting the Avery family?

"I'm going outside to find Gran."

"She might be listening to the minstrels. Your

95

grandfather was a musician. But don't take too long. We still have a lot to do."

Devon nodded. "I won't be long." Her mother had offered a glimpse into her grandfather's past that Devon hadn't heard before. But she'd been down this road before and knew better than to ask her mother to expand. Questions about her father and grandfather were off limits.

****

Devon left the kitchen and meandered down the path toward the booths on the lower grounds. The Dundee family had spared no expense in planning the wedding for their daughter. In addition to the booths filled with vintage fifteenth- and sixteenth-century clothes, there were venders selling small fruit pies and tarts, wax candles, and pottery, as well as jugglers and flame throwers. She spotted her grandmother talking to someone behind one of the pottery booths and waved. The booths backed up to the river and a grouping of beech trees that had lost all their leaves. A layer of cream-white mist clung to the water like clouds of spun sugar and spread to the edge of the booths.

Devon waved again and shouted to get her grandmother's attention as she picked up her long skirts and rushed down the hill. As she ran, she glanced toward the tournament field where she'd seen the knight earlier. The mist had lifted, and workers were setting up the straw stands for an advertised bow and arrow demonstration. The knight was nowhere in sight, and she felt a twinge of regret. Had she imagined him and the words she'd heard in her thoughts?

"Devon," her grandmother shouted. "Over here." Her grandmother waved and motioned Devon to follow her behind a booth packed with painted pottery and place mats imprinted with tapestry scenes.

Why was her grandmother acting so secretive? Devon hugged her grandmother. "Where have you been all day? I've been worried."

"Do you have the cookbook?" Her grandmother was out of breath as though she'd been running, and she was dressed in the same nondescript clothing and head covering as Devon. The strange thing was that she wore contacts to disguise that she had one blue eye and one green, something she'd never done before.

Devon reached into the deep pocket of her long skirt to pull out the cookbook and presented it to her grandmother. "I have been looking everywhere for you. Where have you been?"

Her grandmother cradled the cookbook against her chest. Her face was uncharacteristically somber. Normally, Devon's mother was the serious one and rarely smiled. A winter breeze rattled the branches, and the sound sent shivers chasing over Devon's spine.

"Do you trust me?" her grandmother said.

Her voice held equal parts of panic and fear. It was like that when her grandmother talked about her sister. Devon put her arm around her grandmother's thin shoulders. "Of course I trust you. It's cold. Let's go inside, and I'll make you a nice cup of hot chocolate."

"You can't stop me." Her grandmother released the clasp on the cookbook and a sound like a sigh escaped as she flipped through the pages. "A long time ago your mother donated this cookbook along with others to a charity, and I thought I'd never see it again. Your mother said the book was too dangerous and only brought our family grief." She paused on a page near the back of the cookbook. "Ah. I found the recipe."

"Grandmother, you are not making any sense."

Her grandmother grabbed Devon's arm. "You should come with me. We'll find Charlotte together. Hopefully, you can convince her that it wasn't my fault that I didn't come back for her."

Devon patted her grandmother's hand, trying to calm her. Her grandmother was getting more agitated by the minute.

The story Devon had heard most of her life was that when she was still a child her family had been vacationing in England. While on a tour of one of the castles, Charlotte had wandered off and had never been heard from again. Because she'd never been found, the theory was that she'd drowned in the fast-moving river and been carried out to sea. Devon's grandmother rejected the theory, always believing her sister was still alive. That had been fifteen years ago, and Devon's grandmother had never been the same since.

"I can't do this alone," Devon's grandmother said. "You have more magic in you than you realize. Read aloud the recipe I've indicated, and I'll do the rest. We'll be there in no time."

Devon nodded slowly. "Where are we going?"

"Back in time."

Devon bit down on her lip as her mind screamed as loudly as the kitchen fire alarm had. Only this time her mother wasn't here to turn it off. How her grandmother was acting felt worse than dementia. Her mother had cautioned Devon to be patient and go along with whatever her grandmother asked. Devon doubted her mother had something like this scenario in mind.

But humoring her grandmother seemed like the

safest thing to do, so Devon nodded again. "Sure. I'll go with you."

Her grandmother seemed to relax a little. "Hold the cookbook in both hands and read the recipe for gingerbread. The recipe dates to the time of Queen Elizabeth I, so the language and spelling is reminiscent of Shakespeare's time."

Devon cleared her throat as she read the sixteenth-century recipe. "Take a quart of honey, ginger, cinnamon, powdered pepper, saffron, and grated bread and throw together. Then make it square as though thou wouldst slice it. Bake until…"

Suddenly, a whirling sound blocked out the festival noises as Devon's vision blurred and she felt dizzy. Her grandmother seemed to pull away and dissolve into mist as she shouted Devon's name over and over. The sound was far away and echoed, as though it was coming from a long, dark tunnel.

"Devon. Look for Charlotte. Tell her I'm sorry."

Moments later, her grandmother's words still reverberating through Devon, she awoke to the sound of clattering pots and pans and a mind-splitting headache. She sat on the stone floor in a place that looked like a medieval kitchen. A massive fireplace covered the majority of one wall. Bread baked in red brick ovens, herbs hung from rafters, and men and women worked at a long table in the center of the room making pies and bread.

"Where am I?" Tucking the cookbook back into her deep pocket, she tried to stand. Dizzy, she sank back down on the floor and held her head in her hands.

An older woman knelt beside her and held her finger to her lips. "Please keep your voice low, my sweet girl. I thought I would never see you again." Her smile was gentle and warm. "Devon, I'm your Aunt Charlotte. Welcome to the sixteenth century."

Chapter Two

England, December 20, 1564

Weeks later, with only days before Christmas, the moon's glow streamed into the small room as Devon Avery hid her grandmother's leather-bound cookbook under her pillow for safekeeping.

Lighting her candle on the dying embers in the hearth, she quickened her pace down a dark corridor in the castle, heading toward the massive kitchens on the ground floor. After weeks in this century, she knew her way by heart, but she wasn't supposed to be here. It was an accident. Her grandmother had miscalculated. How many times had she recited those words? A hundred? A thousand?

Repeating them made zero difference. She was stuck here.

She didn't need the candle to chase away the shadows. She needed it for protection. She'd turned down the advances of numerous courtiers and fellow cooks who had never heard a woman utter the word "no."

Avoiding the Neanderthals was a safer solution than giving these men a piece of her mind. Even that conundrum paled when she considered her bigger problem. The penalty for being late for work in the sixteenth century was losing your job and being cast out on the streets.

Devon sped past kitchens separated into specific functions. At three in the morning activity had already begun. Fresh game and vegetables were being unloaded, and fires started in the boiling house and roasting rooms. When she'd first arrived, close to hysteria after realizing where she was, she'd feared she'd be assigned to plucking and gutting. Thankfully, her Aunt Charlotte had mentioned that Devon was a skilled baker. Many viewed Devon as just one of a score of young, single women who created imaginative desserts for the queen and her court. Only Charlotte knew she was from the future.

A loud woof drew her attention and a smile. A brown-and-white Corgi bounded toward her with a boy of eight close behind. She knelt to rub the dog's ears playfully and received a lathered kiss in return. Bran worked in the roasting kitchens and had named his dog Honey.

She nuzzled her face against the dog's soft fur. "Bran, why are you two up so early?"

Bran hugged the dog around the neck. "Honey wanted to see you. Me too."

"I'm glad." She knew the real reason, though, but never let on. This was the same game they played every morning. The boy went to work on an empty stomach. She'd found out by accident and since then always had food for him. She reached into her pocket and brought out cheese and bread she'd saved from her dinner. "I can't eat all of this. Would you like some?"

The boy nodded and wrapped her in a big hug as he accepted the meal. "Thank you."

She stood and tousled the boy's golden curls. "Gobble it down. You don't want to be late."

He nodded again and sped toward the roasting

rooms, this time outpacing Honey.

She smiled, resumed her journey, and turned down the corridor that led to the bake house and pastry rooms until she reached the confectionery room where she was assigned. In less than an hour, more people would descend to prepare the two major meals of the day. When she'd first arrived, she'd felt alone and near sinking into a deep depression. But her work, and meeting people like Charlotte and Bran, had convinced her to make the most of her small blessings. She had a job, a roof over her head, and she hadn't given up hope that one day she would find her way back home. She just had to figure out how to unlock the magic of the cookbook.

Devon entered the confectionery room. The solitary room suited her. She'd never been good with people. They expected too much and asked too many questions. Creating desserts was easier than making friends.

Devon fed bits of kindling to the banked embers under the bake ovens, until the fires sparked to life, and then lit more candles. This was late December, days away from Christmas and dawn a scant few hours away.

Light cheered up the room and illuminated an older woman curled near the hearth asleep. Devon smiled in recognition. Aunt Charlotte had removed her head covering while she slept. The woman's cloud-white hair was shot through with threads of blonde and braided on top of her head like a crown. Charlotte had taken her niece under her wing when Devon arrived, and if she hadn't, Devon would not have survived.

Devon adjusted her head covering that concealed her rebellious curls, knelt, and shook Charlotte's shoulder gently. "Time to wake up." When Charlotte yawned and opened her eyes, Devon smiled. "You stayed here all night again and fell asleep by the fire. You're like the woman in the story of Cinderella and Prince Charming. If you're not careful, I'll start calling you Cinder."

Charlotte yawned again and stretched to a sitting position. "I'm no longer waiting for my prince charming, sweet girl. I'm better suited as the fairy godmother in the story. I prefer a plain man with a good heart."

Devon helped Charlotte to her feet. "Me too. But I don't think they make men like that anymore."

"Still thinking of your mother's idea of the perfect husband, I see. Enough. Let us get to work. I want your opinion on what kept me up all night before that ogre of a chef arrives."

Devon smiled at Charlotte's description of the chef as she let Charlotte lead her over to the long worktable in the center of the room. They had bonded over their mutual dislike of the master chef and nicknamed him Mr. Ogre. Devon reached for an apron from a peg and secured it over the layers of oatmeal-colored clothes she wore. The nondescript clothes were designed to make her look invisible.

Devon had been in a panic when she realized that she had traveled back in time, but Charlotte had eased the transition and taught her how to fit in. Charlotte hadn't said that she had the magic touch, but there had been hints.

Once a batch of fruit pies had burned beyond recognition. The cooks and helpers were in a panic as these were the Queen's favorites and there was no time to bake more. Charlotte stepped in, saying she'd make a sweet honey glaze that would mask the charred dough and overcooked fruit. The results were deemed a miracle, and the Queen had raved the pies were the best she had ever eaten. Devon, recognizing magic when she saw it, knew something else had happened.

There had been other incidents along the way. Sour milk poured out sweet under Charlotte's gaze. A bottomless bowl of honey, and a seemingly endless supply of dried currants and dates. No one paid attention, and if they did question, it was easily explained. In kitchens as large as those at the castle, there was an army of people ordering food. Charlotte simply said she found the items in one of the other kitchens. But when it came to finding a way back to Devon's own time, Charlotte didn't have an answer.

Charlotte gathered broken pieces of gingerbread cookies and gave Devon a handful. "These broke off when I was decorating. Stuff them in your pockets for later. You're looking too thin."

Devon accepted the offering with a nod, then examined the row of gingerbread men Charlotte had decorated during the night. Although only four inches tall, they were lifelike and, at the Queen's request, decorated to resemble the Queen's guard, the Knights of Arthur's Round Table, and the courtiers and guests for the Twelve Days of Christmas celebrations. Charlotte was a gifted artist and used portraits and descriptions to recreate the faces as well as the clothes. Devon was in awe of Charlotte's creations. They looked so real, as though they could spring to life and jump off the table. It had been Devon's idea to arrange the gingerbread men around a gingerbread castle and use the display as a surprise setting for the Queen's table.

"As always, they are beautiful," Devon said. "You have a way of bringing out the best qualities in a portrait.

You even made the Queen's alchemist, John Dee, look pleasant. He always looks like he is in a bad mood."

"Alchemist is a safe word to describe the man. John Dee is a puzzle I'm not sure I want to solve. And as for his bad mood, he has a right to it. He risks much when he makes star charts for the Queen's entertainment. Mr. Dee is a sorcerer, is my guess, and the Queen would do well to be cautious."

"You don't have to worry about the Queen. She is a smart woman, and I know she will be pleased with your creations. Do you need me to make more gingerbread men? I don't see ones for King Eric of Sweden or Charles, Archduke of Austria."

Charlotte shook her head as she moved the gingerbread men onto a platter. "No need. The Queen said she didn't want to see their likeness. She tires of her suitors. They are all such a bore." Charlotte chuckled. "I heard one of her ladies in waiting quote those exact words, saying that the Queen wanted a quieter, less political Christmas this year. With that in mind, she commanded I decorate several versions of Robert Dudley, Earl of Leicester, with clothes in a variety of color combinations that would match her own."

"That's romantic. Too bad the Queen and the Earl never got together."

Charlotte heaved a sigh. "I agree. Sad indeed. The Queen missed her opportunity. When a person finds love, they should hold onto it and never let go. Well, enough about the Queen. I will set the gingerbread men in the cooler until you are ready to place them around your gingerbread castle." Charlotte paused. "Tell me again the type of suitor you would conjure if you had the skill?"

Devon held her breath, as her gaze focused on the entrance. If they were overheard... These were dangerous times for people who were different. Deadly if you were branded a witch. "Please. Lower your voice. I've told you over and over. I'm not like my mother and grandmother. I don't have any powers. I can't conjure or cast spells."

"So you've mentioned. And you didn't answer my question, sweet girl. What kind of man do you desire?"

"We've been over that before."

"One more time. Humor a cranky old woman."

Devon hugged her waist. "You are neither old nor cranky, and you understand me far better than my mother does."

Charlotte reached for Devon's hand and squeezed. "I believe your mother only does what she thinks is best. I've often said that motherhood is training for becoming a grandmother. About my question..."

Devon smiled. "You won't let go of a question once it's asked? Fine. I wish for a man with a generous and kind heart and who thinks of others before he thinks of himself. Which means I'm asking for the impossible, and I might as well wish for a purple unicorn with rainbow sprinkles."

Charlotte floated a cloth over her tray of gingerbread men. "Nothing is impossible in my kitchen."

Chapter Three

Moments later, men and women poured into the kitchens as though summoned by an invisible alarm. A few nodded greetings, as each went to a workstation to begin preparations. Mr. Ogre had arrived as well, although people only called him that behind his back. He reminded Devon of the description of the Tweedledum character from *Alice in Wonderland*. Mr. Ogre's real name was Mr. Lum. He looked puffed up and boiling mad as he argued with Charlotte over the quantity of currants to add to the pies. The arguments between Mr. Lum and Charlotte were an everyday occurrence, with Charlotte always on the winning side. There was a sweetness about it that bordered on foreplay, but Devon would never dare bring that to Charlotte's attention.

Good grief. Why was romance so much on her mind lately? She blamed Charlotte and her question on what kind of man Devon needed…or was it wanted? The two words always confused Devon. Weren't they the same thing?

She refocused her thoughts. She didn't have time for thoughts of romance. She needed to finish the gingerbread castle that was to be used as a centerpiece on the Queen's table. Technically, gingerbread houses weren't popular until the Brothers Grimm published their collection of folklore in 1812, which included the story of Hansel and Gretel discovering a house made of cookies, candies, and cakes in the forest. But since the Queen was credited with instructing that gingerbread men be created to resemble guests, Devon thought this might be a case where the history books miscalculated the impact of gingerbread by a century or two.

The problem was that she had promised she could build a scaled-down version of a castle by Christmas Day, and she was having construction issues. She couldn't get the proportions correct, and she'd made the mistake of submitting a drawing to the Queen.

The air filled with the scents of spices and herbs, gifted from the travels of the Queen's merchants and privateers, as cooks began preparing desserts. The variety of smells and textures was as endless as the imagination. Cinnamon, cloves, and nutmeg were secured in glass jars, while mint, basil, and rosemary plants perched on windowsills in neat rows, and lavender hung in fat bundles from the rafters to dry.

She rolled out the gingerbread dough she was preparing at Queen Elizabeth's request as her thoughts turned toward her mother. The two seemed to have something in common. Both appeared to have a hard outer shell. Her mother liked to compare herself to meringue cookies—hard on the outside and sweet on the inside. Devon had rarely seen her mother's sweet side after her father's death but hadn't argued the point. As a result, she was closer to her grandmother and shared her passion for researching old recipes. Even before traveling back in time, Devon had researched what foods were available in the fifteenth and sixteenth centuries. Much to her dismay, chocolate wouldn't be in wide use until much later.

Men's shouts and a child's scream sliced through

the kitchen's routine. The hum of work and conversation ceased as though someone had pressed a pause button. Pots and utensils clattered as people turned toward the sound, and Mr. Lum and Charlotte stopped in mid argument and also turned toward the source of the disturbance.

In the roasting rooms, something crashed to the floor. Then came the metallic sound of skillets striking stone, followed by thuds and shattering noises as pottery exploded against walls. More shouts. All around Devon, people in the kitchen huddled together and backed further from the door. They were frozen, fearful of moving. Violence rarely reached this part of the castle. Intrigue, perhaps, affairs, absolutely, but violence was not common. Devon had heard of the time when there had been an attempted poisoning, but the culprit had been found quickly and executed in the Tower of London. The stain never reached the kitchens.

A child screamed again. This time Devon made out the word, "Stop."

Shivers chased up Devon's spine. The child sounded as young as eight or nine, maybe younger. She'd seen children working in the kitchens, fetching wood, food, and doing odd jobs. In the twenty-first century forcing children this young to work from dawn to dusk was illegal and a violation of child labor law. But this was the sixteenth century and a different time. People from her time thought children were forced to endure these harsh conditions because they weren't as cherished and loved. Not true. It wasn't lack of love—it was about survival. The more people in a family who worked meant more food on the table.

Devon dusted off her hands and moved from the

table. She would not stand by while someone was in danger.

Charlotte grabbed her arm. "Where are you going?" Her voice was low and strained.

Devon removed Charlotte's hand from her arm. "I'm just going to see what's going on. I'll be right back."

Charlotte blocked her path. "Leave it be."

"I can't."

Devon walked around Charlotte and headed toward the roasting rooms. Chaos greeted her. The room looked as though it had been turned upside down by a giant. Tables and benches were overturned or upended. Pottery had been broken, and all sizes and shapes of cooking utensils scattered over floors and surfaces. Two men, swords raised, faced each other in the center of the room.

At first glance they were equal in height and strength and in their late twenties or early thirties. Neither looked like they worked in the kitchens, nor did they dress like courtiers, in silks, jewels, and expensive fur trims. They stood like warriors, in earth-toned long trousers and simple shirts. Their skin was weathered, their eyes angry.

"The boy is not yours to abuse." The warrior who spoke commanded the attention of all in the kitchen, his voice clear and as loud as a building storm that only warned once before it attacked.

Her attention drawn to the man who'd spoken, Devon stepped into the roasting room and moved to stand against the wall. She searched the room for the boy the man had mentioned and noticed Bran cowering under a table a short distance from where she stood. His face was bloodied, and his shirt torn. She covered her mouth to stifle a scream and focused once more on the man who'd spoken.

Second glance told her that he was more than he had at first appeared. The man who had spoken had tied back his dark hair as though ready for battle. There was a scar that creased his eyebrow, his jaw was set, and his eyes were hard. He stood straight and tall and confident. The sword held out toward his opponent had not wavered, while the other man's sword trembled from the weight and strain.

"This is not your fight," the other man said. "This boy belongs to me."

"No man owns another," said the man with the scar. "Release him or fight me. Those are your choices."

"Who are you that you challenge me? I have the right to know."

"Sir Graham," the man with the scar said. "I am a visiting knight who honors the code to protect the weak and defenseless." He lifted his sword a little higher until the tip of the blade was inches from the man's throat.

Devon glanced toward Bran, who shook so much she imagined she could hear his teeth chattering. What would happen to him once the fighting started? If she were a betting person, her money was on Sir Graham. But anything could happen in the heat of a battle, and she didn't know if the other man had friends who would rush the knight when the fighting started.

She needed to get Bran to safety.

She edged closer to Bran and knelt, whistling low to get his attention. "Come with me. We don't have much time."

Bran spared a glance toward the two men and nodded, crawling out from under the table. She scooped him in her arms. He was skin and bones and clung to her as she turned and fled from the room.

Chapter Four

Sir Graham, after rendering unconscious the man who had attacked the young lad, sheathed his sword, and glanced in the direction he had seen the rescuer go with the boy. He could not believe his good fortune. She was the woman he had been searching for.

The roasting room had gone back to the way it had been before his arrival. Men hauled the slaughtered carcasses of boar and deer to tables for preparation. Others diced potatoes and greens or stoked the fires in the twin hearths. As he left, no one spoke to him, and they walked around him as though he were a statue. Such behavior was to be expected.

Even before gaining the battle scars that crisscrossed his face, his appearance had never inspired romantic ballads. He was taller and broader than most, a hard man with hard lines. He was feared, and it worked to his advantage. He always succeeded in his quest, but never had it been this easy, and that worried him.

His search for the woman with one blue eye and one green had led him to this castle. He recognized her from the description and her distinctive eyes. Her quick thinking and bravery had been unexpected, but it would not deter him from his duty.

He followed the way he had seen her take. Once outside, he heard a dog's bark and recognized the sound. It had been that sound that led him to the boy and his attacker.

The woman knelt beside the boy, and when Graham approached, the animal barked a greeting and ran toward him with the boy close behind. He remembered how the dog had defended the boy, a fearless soldier in the face of danger. Even when the man had kicked the dog out of the way, the animal had not given up, but nipped at the man's heels. The commotion had alerted Graham to the seriousness of what was happening.

He glanced from the boy and dog toward the woman. She had turned as if aware of Graham's attention. Concern turned to relief on her lovely face in a heartbeat.

In the next beat she was on her feet, running toward him. Her head covering slipped loose, releasing waves of hair the color of a harvest bonfire. She reached for his hand, pumping it with both of hers. Taken off guard, he was rendered speechless.

"My name's Devon," she said with a musical lilt to her voice that evoked the sound of water dancing over a rock wall. "And the boy you saved is Bran. You were kind to help Bran and his dog. I can't thank you enough."

He was spellbound by her voice as she went on and on, talking about his bravery in facing the boy's attacker. He heard only a fraction of what she said. He was mesmerized by not only her voice but the color of her eyes. He had described them as one blue and one green, but they were much more. They were rimmed with a thin band of cobalt blue, and specks of silver glittered in each eye like stars on a velvet night.

The woman spoke to Graham as though he were not a giant but a person of an acceptable height. She spoke to him as though his appearance was not scarred but pleasant to the eye. Did she see beneath the mask?

She had stopped talking and yet still held his hand between hers. Her hands were a woman's hands—small, graceful, and capable of boundless strength and courage. She looked at him expectantly. She wanted him to respond. What did she expect him to say?

He had not done anything he considered out of the ordinary. He was a knight, pledged to protect the weak and innocent. Yet he knew she expected a response.

He understood how to react to people who feared him. This was a new experience. He rehearsed his words. He wanted to ask why she did not fear him. He wanted to ask if she knew why he felt as though he could listen to her voice until the end of time. He discarded the questions for neutral ground.

"Thank you for your kind words, but it is a knight's sworn duty to protect." His voice growled out like a beast, but it was too late to draw it back.

She did not startle or jump in reaction to the sound of his voice. In truth, she seemed amused.

"You look hungry," she said. "Come with me." She turned and retraced her steps to the kitchens as though expecting him to follow.

She was right. He was hungry. Starving. But it was more than hunger. It was desire.

What strangeness had come over him? It were as though he was bewitched. He felt as though he would follow her anywhere, deny her nothing, give her the world. If she wanted him to jump off the Cliffs of Moher, all she would have to do was ask.

He scrubbed his face with his hand, attempting to banish the strange thoughts. There was no time for distractions. He had been sent to find the woman with one blue eye and one green and bring her to Lord Basil in exchange for his mother's freedom. He could not fail.

Chapter Five

Devon led the way to the confectionery kitchen, her heart pounding with each step that echoed down the corridor. It was well past midday, and cooks were hard at work preparing meals for the Queen and her court. Tonight's dinner would not be as grand as the one served on Christmas Day, as the rules of Advent forbade meat and dairy on certain days, but the cooks still managed to produce a feast. Preparation was underway for boiled mussels, stewed oysters with thyme, and carp that was baked with diced prunes, nutmeg, cumin, and ginger.

Bran walked beside her, chattering away to his dog, Honey. Every now and then Honey would woof in response to one of Bran's comments. Bran seemed unfazed by what had happened earlier. She, on the other hand, was a mess.

She'd seen plenty of knights in shiny armor over the past few weeks, and some were swoon worthy. Sir Graham, however, was on a different level. Although he towered over everyone in the room, he wasn't movie-star or model handsome. He had that quiet, you-can-lean-on-me look in his eyes that made her knees go weak and her heart race out of control.

"Is the knight still behind us?" she said to Bran, strangely out of breath.

Bran glanced over his shoulder and nodded.

"Good," she said on a release of air and then didn't

know why that mattered, or why she felt safer.

She had operated on adrenaline when she'd first heard Bran's scream for help. Making sure he was safe had been paramount. She'd relaxed a little when she saw this giant of a man swoop in and save the day. She'd thought she'd seen him glance her way when she left with Bran but hadn't been positive. She never dreamed he'd follow them outside.

But he had.

One minute she was making sure Bran was all right and the next the knight had appeared as though out of thin air. He was so tall that she'd had to lean back to see his face. She'd focused on his eyes, a trick she'd learned from her grandmother. Because Devon had one blue and one green, she had endured scores of teasings as a child. As a result, a person's eyes were the first feature she noticed.

Her grandmother had been the one who had comforted her and dried her tears when kids at school teased her about the color of her eyes. Her mother worked long hours and was rarely home. When Devon would come home from a rough day at school, her grandmother would bring out her cookbooks and let Devon chose a cookie recipe to bake. It was her grandmother who taught her the old saying that the eyes were a window into the soul. She would also say that you could tell a lot about a person if you concentrated on their eyes and ignored the rest of their appearance. In those times they spent together, her grandmother shared not only her secrets on baking but also how to read the emotions reflected in a person's eyes.

Maybe her grandmother's advice was the reason she couldn't get her impression of the knight's eyes out of her thoughts, as though they had been imprinted forever on her heart.

His eyes were nutmeg brown with specks of gold dust. They were kind eyes. Gorgeous eyes. The type that belonged to a person who would listen and think of others' needs before his own. His gaze reflected a gentle nature beneath the hard exterior. Bran and his dog had recognized this as well and had run without fear to the knight when he'd followed them outside. In the garden, when the knight had glanced toward Bran and the dog, his eyes had reflected much in a short span of time.

His expression had filled with concern, and then anger toward the man who'd tormented Bran. It had then shifted to relief when he realized Bran and his dog were both okay. She saw all those emotions in a blink of time—and more. A deep sadness held him, and, in that moment, she wished she could be the person he would trust enough to help him banish the sadness from his eyes.

Then the knight had glanced her way, and her breath had caught. She saw that he admired her for her bravery and for helping Bran. She saw confusion but did not understand its source. Then she saw something that made her body warm and her face flush. She saw attraction, and felt its pull on her as well.

As she neared the castle's confectionary kitchen, she slowed her pace, not wanting to share the knight with anyone else. It was an irrational thought. He was not hers. The clatter of pots and pans, the aroma of baking breads, and the hum of conversation, laced with intermittent laughter…it all intruded, forcing her to stop.

Bran and Honey raced into the kitchen, but Devon stayed behind. The knight had hesitated as well and stood beside her, so close that all she would have had to do was move a fraction of an inch to touch him. "Thank you again for saving Bran," she said to the knight. She raised her head and was lost in the warmth of his gaze.

Long, dark eyelashes framed his eyes as he nodded. "Your bravery was greater than mine, Lady Devon."

Somehow the knight had captured her hand and had pressed it to his lips for a kiss. His mouth lingered, and his touch sent hot shivers chasing over her skin. The kiss on her hand lingered long enough for her eyes to meet his, and long enough for her to know that he wanted to take her into his arms and never let her go.

She heard Honey bark and pulled her hand from the knight's, averting her gaze. It was as though a strange enchantment had possessed them, but now it lifted, like mist chased by a summer breeze.

The kitchen was as she'd left it, with the exception that more workers had arrived. No one took notice of her, but then the knight crossed over the threshold. When he did, all activity stopped.

Charlotte, the first to greet him and welcome him into the kitchen, dusted her hands on her apron and rushed to greet the knight. She gave a slight curtsy. "Sir Graham, your name is on everyone's lips. We heard what you did for young Bran, and we are most grateful. We are at your disposal. Is there something you desire?"

His gaze snapped to Devon's, then back to scan the kitchen as though searching for an answer to Charlotte's question. His attention settled on the workstation where Charlotte had been decorating more gingerbread cookies. The confusion in his expression returned. "I…"

"I believe that Sir Graham is hungry," Devon blurted. Her face had flushed under his gaze, and she needed a distraction. She didn't know if the knight planned to bolt, but she didn't want to take the chance. She ignored the little *Why do you care?* comment in her head. "I promised Sir Graham a meal."

"An easy promise to keep," Charlotte said. "Devon, please show Sir Graham to the room off the kitchen, and I will prepare a feast for our honored guest."

"Can Honey and I come too?" Bran said, his face turned toward Charlotte in a hopeful smile.

"Yes, dear boy. There is enough for you and your loyal friend as well. Would you like to help me?" With Bran's nod and Honey's bark, Charlotte left to gather food on trays, leaving Devon alone with the knight.

The knight's brows twisted together as though trying to solve a problem. "You are not the lady of the manor. You are a serving maid, then?" He seemed pleased with the revelation.

She smiled. "I prefer apprentice cook, but yes, I am definitely not the lady of the manor, or anything remotely close. Queen Elizabeth and her court are visiting the castle for the Twelve Days of Christmas celebrations."

"That will change everything," he said more to himself than to her.

Chapter Six

Conversation hummed around Devon like bees in a meadow at the height of summer. A short time ago, Bran had finished eating the meal Charlotte had prepared for him and had run out carrying a drawstring purse filled with gold coins Sir Graham had given him. According to Bran, the knight wanted to make sure Bran no longer worked in the kitchens and planned to visit his family to make sure they were well taken care of. The knight's generosity took everyone by surprise. As soon as Bran and the dog left to play outside, the speculation on the knight's wealth and origins were all the people in the kitchen could talk about.

The speculation that Sir Graham must be as rich as a king, to give so generous a purse to a child, fueled the gossip in the kitchen. The knight must own numerous castles, one of the men who brought wood in for the bake ovens suggested, or manor houses and a fleet of merchant ships, Mr. Lum added. The women baking pies insisted that the reason the knight's face was scarred was because he had been a pirate in the exotic seven seas, where fighting was a way of life and treasure easily obtained. They laughed that a man's scars were easily ignored when his purse was full of gold coins.

These same women had brought trays of pies and pastries to the knight. Devon heard their giggles and laughter, and occasionally, she heard the knight speak, but his voice was too low to make out the words.

Not that she cared, she told herself, and she certainly wasn't jealous.

She snagged a baked gingerbread square from the tray and applied frosting along one end, then attached it on the standing gingerbread wall. Distracted with thoughts of the knight, she applied it so forcefully a corner broke off. She mumbled under her breath and tried to refocus.

"What are you building?"

The knight's deep voice startled her. She hadn't seen or heard him approach. He stood so close she could smell the scent of leather and spice and feel the warmth of his breath on the back of her neck. Her mind and fingers went numb as the gingerbread wall she held slipped out of her grasp and tumbled to the ground.

In a daze, she stared at the broken pieces, not knowing whether to laugh or cry. Maybe she'd do both. All that work...

"I apologize for startling you," the knight said in a hushed tone as he scooped the gingerbread pieces off the floor and put them onto the worktable. "Is it possible for you to bake more?"

She zeroed in on the broken pieces on the worktable. She was annoyed with her reaction to the knight's sudden approach and the women flirting with him. Most of all, she was just annoyed. She was acting jealous when she barely knew the guy. What was wrong with her?

She retrieved one of the pieces of gingerbread and took a bite to calm her libido. She needed the sugar high. "Yes, I can make more."

He brushed her shoulder as he reached for one of the gingerbread pieces on the table. "The women said you were building a replica of a castle. I have some experience. I was a stone mason and helped add a wing to a castle for a Scottish nobleman."

Devon nodded slowly. The knight was trying to lead them back to neutral ground. At least one of them was acting rationally. She ventured a smile. "I welcome the help. If you don't mind my asking, Sir Graham, how did you go from a stone mason to a knight?"

A shadow passed over his eyes, turning them the color of earth after a winter rainstorm. She didn't like the change. It made his eyes look sad.

"One of the walls collapsed while the owner was inspecting the construction, and I managed to pull Lord Basil to safety." The knight paused. "He was grateful and offered me the opportunity to fight for him. I was a skilled stone mason, but better on the battlefield. My journey to knighthood was a longer story. Please call me Graham."

"Graham," she said, her heart fluttering so fast she put her hand over her chest to catch her breath. "You offered to help. I'm grateful. Where should we start?"

"A proper castle will need a courtyard around the keep, battlements, arrow slits, portcullis, and a moat and draw bridge."

His gaze settled on hers, his eyes a light cinnamon brown that warmed her to her toes and sent shivers over her skin. She liked this shade very much.

She pulled an empty bowl toward her. "I'll need to make more gingerbread. We might be here all night."

"I have nowhere else I would rather be than here with you."

"Sir Graham, please pardon the interruption," Mr. Lum said. "Lord Basil has arrived and requests your presence."

Chapter Seven

The day blended into night, leaving Devon feeling alone and adrift as she set the last batch of gingerbread cookies on the table to cool. The kitchen had been scrubbed clean and everyone had left. Just this morning, she'd relished her alone time. Graham had changed that paradigm for her. He made her feel alive again, hope again, maybe for the first time in her life.

She'd never been attracted to a man this fast before, and it was unsettling. Her grandmother had volunteered that when Avery women fell in love, they fell fast, and they fell hard. She refused to believe that had happened to her. And if it had, why now? Why Graham, and why had it happened when she was hundreds of years in the past?

She covered the gingerbread castle and lit a candle to light her way to her room, deciding to take a detour to check on the decorations in the Great Hall. She was curious about the Christmas preparations, and it would get her mind off Graham.

Easier said than done.

She reached the Great Hall and let the images that greeted her push her troubling thoughts into the background. Christmas was her favorite time of year, and living in Elizabethan times, when it was less about the presents and more about the season for rejoicing, rekindled her love of Christmas.

Ropes of glistening ivy and bright red berries framed the entrance to the Great Hall. Keeping to the shadows, Devon crept inside for a quick peek. Even this late at night, preparations were in progress for the dinner and After Party on Christmas evening.

The morning and afternoon of Christmas Day would be devoted to prayer and church services. In the evening the merriment would begin celebrating the Twelve Days of Christmas, to culminate on Epiphany, January sixth. Dinner on Christmas would be elaborate, but it was the Queen's After Party that Devon was excited to witness. Devon's gingerbread castle would be the focal point, and when dismantled, the pieces would be served on plates made from what was called sugar-glass and tinted in reds and greens.

Commotion drew Devon's attention to the entrance. Workmen were busy bringing in more tables and chairs, and one of the men motioned for her to leave. She'd learned that you were given only one warning and hurried from the Great Hall in the direction of the servants' quarters.

Charlotte had shown her ways to travel unseen from one wing to another in a short span of time through secret passageways constructed behind the walls, but she had cautioned they were to be used in emergency situations only.

When Devon reached her destination, she headed toward the room she shared with Charlotte. Charlotte hadn't arrived yet, and the room was pitch black. Devon lit another candle and sank down on the small bed. Charlotte had left a traditional gingerbread cookie on the nightstand for Devon. He was adorable, with his round eyes, nose, and cute upturned mouth all made of white frosting.

Devon smiled at Charlotte's kind gesture and stretched. She'd been awake since dawn and should be bone weary. Normally, she'd fall into bed with barely the strength to wash and change into a nightgown. Was the mysterious knight the cause of her nervous energy? She couldn't get him out of her thoughts.

She removed her head covering and shook her hair loose, massaging her neck as she tucked her legs under her. There was something about the knight and the way he looked at her that made her feel as though she were the most important person in a room. She'd never experienced that feeling before. That she was attracted to him was undeniable.

She stretched out on the bed and felt her grandmother's cookbook under her pillow. She sat up again and retrieved it, staring at the green leather cover and gold clasp. She'd opened the clasp many times since she'd arrived, hoping she could duplicate what had happened to her, only to experience disappointment. She was stuck in this century.

But it was her ritual at night to open it and think of her mother and grandmother, so she unlatched the clasp and opened the book. A shoosh of air escaped, and the powerful scent of crushed cloves exploded around her. Odd. That had never happened before. She waved her hand to disperse the aroma.

The gingerbread cookie on the plate sat up.

Startled, she screamed, dropped the book, and scooted back against the wall.

The gingerbread man flopped back down on the plate as though nothing had happened.

Chapter Eight

The afternoon of Christmas Eve arrived but felt like just another day to the kitchen staff. The rich aroma of gingerbread laced with cinnamon, cloves, cardamom, and nutmeg warmed the air as Devon rolled out more dough. It smelled like the Christmas seasons where she, her mother, and grandmother had conducted marathon baking sessions as they prepared for the holidays. Back then, they only had the Gingerbread House Bakery, and catering weddings hadn't been on their to-do list. Devon knew those memories were the reason she loved making gingerbread. The smells and working with the dough brought back some of the happiest memories of her life.

It was also the first time she'd seen her grandmother animate a gingerbread man.

Had she been more tired last night than she'd thought and only imagined she'd magically brought a gingerbread man to life? How was that possible? She'd never shown magical abilities before. No, it had happened, and her fingers still tingled where they had touched the cookbook.

Feeling more protective of the cookbook after the incident last night, she'd brought it with her and placed it on the cupboard shelf in the kitchen, not wanting to let it out of her sight. Something strange had happened, and until she figured out what it was, she wanted to keep the cookbook close.

Graham had arrived a short time ago to help her finish the gingerbread castle, and his presence caused a stir until Mr. Lum ordered everyone to go about their business as though they didn't have a knight of Graham's stature helping in the kitchens.

She slid a glance in Graham's direction and received a smile as a reward. Her face warmed, wanting this day to never end. He had removed his tunic and rolled up the sleeves of his shirt to withdraw a tray of gingerbread from the oven. The muscles on his forearms corded as he added more wood to the fire in the ovens.

The man was powerfully built, with broad shoulders and seemingly limitless strength. From the way he dealt with the man who had bullied Bran, it was easy to imagine Graham on the battlefield. He was a man you wanted as a friend, not a foe. And yet he was a man of many layers. He had a creative side that had taken her by surprise.

It felt right somehow that she was creating a gingerbread castle with Graham. She'd known him a short time and yet felt as though they'd known each other much longer. She'd been drawn to him because of his kindness toward Bran. Then the nutmeg warmth of his eyes and the deep tone of his voice intensified her attraction.

Reluctantly, she resumed her work and concentrated on the construction of her gingerbread castle. She had the back and side walls erected. She'd used royal icing to glue the sides together but had had to improvise the ingredients. Royal icing consisted of egg whites and sugar. That wasn't a problem, but the key ingredient was cream of tartar, which wouldn't be available for several hundred years. Instead of cream of tartar, she'd substituted white vinegar, a trick she'd learned from her grandmother.

When the inside gingerbread walls were cooled down enough, Devon used tinted frosting to create miniature tapestries that included flower fairies and unicorns frolicking in pastoral settings. She'd learned how to make the variety of tints from Charlotte. There were pots of yellow and gold made from saffron, reds and pinks from dried rose petals, blues from blackberries and mulberries, greens from parsley and herbs, browns from cinnamon, and purple from violets.

Devon savored the intimacy of the time they were spending together as she placed the sections of gingerbread dough Graham had cut into two-inch-wide strips on a tray. When they were cooled, they planned to use icing to glue the strips together into cylinders to create the castle's towers. She very much wanted to know this man better. More than that, she wanted him in her arms.

They had worked well together, sometimes laughing over spilled flour or growing serious as they planned the construction pieces they would need to bring their joint creation to life. Queen Elizabeth's Coat of Arms included the images of a lion and a winged dragon, so Devon decided to make these animals the same size as the gingerbread noblemen and knights Charlotte had created.

Time over the last few hours had flowed as though in a dream as Devon worked beside Graham, creating the gingerbread castle. They spoke very little and seemed to anticipate each other's needs. Gradually, people left the kitchen for their homes. Charlotte had gone as well but promised to return later.

Devon stretched, only now realizing she'd been on her feet all day. Where had the day gone? She handed Graham the tray of gingerbread sections. "While they bake, would you like to take a break and go outside while the dough cooks?"

His nod seemed to speak more than words, as though he too hadn't wanted this day to end. He opened the door, and a whisper of snow drifted toward her on a chilled breeze. After the warmth of the kitchen, the difference in temperature was a stark contrast.

She shivered and hugged her waist, already missing the warmth and smells of the kitchen. "Maybe this wasn't such a good idea."

His arms went around her, holding her against him and sheltering her from the cold. "We can go back inside if you desire." His breath smelled of cinnamon and cloves.

She felt the rumble of his voice and the steady beat of his heart as she snuggled within his embrace. His heat was like a banked fire that warmed but also promised to burn if you ventured too close. And more than anything in her life she wanted to burn. "No, this is perfect right where we are."

She knew nothing about him. He was a puzzle of conflicting pieces in a world where every waking hour for her had been a struggle to survive and to understand her place in a world she didn't understand.

In this moment, with Graham, she felt safe, normal, doing familiar things. Intellectually she knew she was still in the sixteenth century, but today there had been long stretches of time when working beside Graham she had imagined they were in her grandmother's bakery, rolling out dough and decorating cookies together. She wanted to hold onto that feeling as long as possible.

His lips parted on a sigh as his arms pulled her against the length of his hard body. "Devon…"

She knew he was asking if he could kiss her. She barely knew the man, and yet he didn't feel like a stranger. It felt as though they had been lifelong friends who just realized what they felt for each other went deeper then friendship.

"Yes," she whispered and rose to kiss him.

****

Long, exquisite moments later, Devon drew back from the kiss on a current of sweet honey and spices. Lightheaded, she clung to Graham, never wanting to let go of him. "I feel I've known you…"

"…a lifetime," he finished, kissing her on the top of her head.

She turned in his arms, with her back against his chest, and gazed at the night sky. "The stars…" She sighed. "There are so many. I've never seen them so bright and so close. It's almost as though I could reach up and gather them in my hand. They are beautiful."

The beat of his heart seemed to pick up a few notches. "The night sky has never been a source of beauty for me until tonight. I enjoy seeing it from your eyes. The stars' function was to direct me on the right path."

He sounded practical, but his kiss showed another side of him, the side full of passion and desire. "I don't think I could identify a constellation. I just think the stars are pretty, like silver sprinkles on a chocolate cookie."

He swept a curl behind her ear and kissed the nape of her neck, sending warm shivers over her skin. "How do you find your way if not by studying the stars?"

She leaned against him. So this was what it felt like to be in the arms of someone you desired. She could stand with him like this forever. Still, she held back. He was a man from a superstitious time. She couldn't very well tell him about GPS. It would sound like magic and sorcery. She dodged to answer, "I don't travel much anymore. How about you?"

"I travel more than I would like." His voice held a faraway quality, as though he were remembering with regret the places he had visited.

Had her mother reached that same conclusion? Had she regretted that the cost of building an Avery empire meant she'd missed precious time with her daughter? Devon fought back her own regret. Maybe her mother had not made an effort, but neither had she.

Devon pressed the heel of her hand against her eyes to banish the thoughts and the cold, hard reality that she might never have the chance to change things between her and her mother. She was lost back in time, not knowing if she would ever return.

She felt Graham watching her and offering her a smile to banish her dark mood. She turned and embraced his smile and drew its magic around her. "You mentioned you travel a lot. Do knights like you fight for someone, or do you pick and choose your battles?"

"Both. I have fought for someone else's cause as well as chosen a fight I believed worth fighting. Most of that is in my past. In the present, I return lost or stolen things to their rightful owners."

Had he read her thoughts? She'd referred to herself as lost, and the way he talked about finding lost things sounded more like it was people he found, not things. And there was something else about those words…

135

They rolled over her, crushing the breath from her lungs. She'd heard those words before from the knight she'd seen the same day she'd received the cookbook from the shopkeeper and traveled back in time. It couldn't be a coincidence. The knight had been shrouded in a silver mist and had disappeared before she could distinguish his features. But she had never forgotten the words he'd spoken.

I find lost things.

Were Sir Graham and the knight the same person?

Impossible. And yet…

She gathered the threads of courage around her like a cloak. She was about to accuse a man she barely knew, a man she was attracted to and with whom she had shared a kiss, of traveling forward in time. Should she be suspicious that he hadn't mentioned it, when she'd kept from him the fact she'd time traveled, as well?

She had to tread lightly. These were superstitious times, and she'd be willing to bet that admitting you were a time traveler was akin to admitting to witchcraft. She took a deep breath and plunged forward cautiously.

"What you said about finding lost things. I've heard a knight say those words before. Any chance there are other knights that do what you do?"

"There are no other knights like me." His statement was not bravado, his tone said it as fact.

She sensed her next questions would be more difficult to frame. She couldn't very well ask him if he'd traveled forward in time. That would be too risky. "Have we met before? I mean, I think I saw you, or a knight dressed like you before. He also said he found lost things. It was a long way away, and I never saw his face, but is there a chance you have seen me before?"

She waited for his answer. Saw the shift in the color of his eyes from light to dark. His hesitation dragged on long enough that she knew whatever answer he gave would be a lie.

He blew on his hands to ward against a chill she sensed he didn't feel. "No. I have never seen you before."

Warning bells went off in her head at the same moment she smelled the smoke. Her gingerbread cookies had caught on fire.

Chapter Ten

The fires in the kitchen ovens had died down and the chill in the air turned glacial as Devon watched Graham leave. She reminded herself she'd asked him to go. She'd made some excuse that she wanted to finish alone as that was how she worked best. A lie. But then, she suspected he had lied as well. Was Graham the knight she'd seen in the future the day she'd traveled back in time?

She'd used the last of the dough to replace the batch of burned gingerbread and didn't have the mental strength to make more. If he was the knight she'd seen, what was the connection?

First things first. She had to finish the gingerbread castle centerpiece before Christmas morning. There was an unbroken rule in Queen Elizabeth's court. If you made a promise to the Queen, you'd better keep it or risk consequences, not only to yourself but for those around you. The gingerbread castle was only three quarters of the way finished. The burned tower pieces had been designed to complete the last section of the castle. If only she had the magical skill to create something from nothing.

"I thought I would find you here," Charlotte said, reaching for her apron on the wooden peg on the wall. "Where is that handsome knight, Sir Graham?" Charlotte examined the gingerbread castle, bending down to get a closer look. She drew a breath. "Interesting. You say you worked on this with your knight?" She laughed softly. "Well done. You and your knight have done beautiful work together. The Queen will be pleased."

"I sent Graham away." The ominous tone in her voice fit her mood. She had dropped her guard and opened her heart only to discover that the person she was attracted to was harboring a secret. She squared her shoulders, keeping her voice as bland as cookie dough without flavorings. "The castle is unfinished. The tower section burned, and I've run out of dough. A perfect storm."

Charlotte paused, her expression focused on Devon as intently as it had been on the gingerbread castle. "I personally find storms invigorating. Are you going to tell me what's wrong?"

"I burnt a batch of gingerbread."

"I can see that. And…"

"Graham and I kissed, and then I sent him away."

"You did what?" Charlotte glanced between the gingerbread castle and Devon. "Well, ask him to come back."

"I don't want to talk about it."

Charlotte picked up one of the burned pieces of gingerbread, then set it down with a sigh. "Ignoring a problem, hoping it will go away…" She shook her head. "You are so much like my sister. Well, let's focus on the centerpiece then, shall we?" She peered at the castle, its tapestries, portraits of past kings and queens of England, and the crest of Queen Elizabeth I that Devon had painted on the gingerbread interior walls. Charlotte glanced toward Devon with a sly smile. "These paintings are magnificent and lifelike. Did you intend to animate the fairies?"

"What are you talking about?" Devon walked over to take a closer look and then sucked in her breath. Tiny, winged fairies fluttered in the trees Devon had painted on the gingerbread walls. Devon straightened and rubbed her eyes. "The fairies look alive. I didn't want to say anything earlier, but a short time ago I animated the gingerbread cookie you left on the nightstand beside my bed. What do you think it means?"

"It means your gift has awakened. But we will have to be careful. People in this century are afraid of what they do not understand. Hopefully, the fairies will behave themselves and keep out of sight. I'll add my gingerbread nobles and knights in the center. If only I had my sister's skill, I could make them dance." She tilted her head to the side. "Maybe you have inherited my sister's skill."

Devon shook her head. "You keep saying my gift has awakened, but I have no idea how I made the cookies animate. For all we know, it could have been Graham."

"I don't think so. However, I suspect your knight's appearance awakened your gifts."

"You keep calling Graham 'my knight.' He's not…mine. And what does he have to do with my gifts?"

"Everything. I was waiting for you to fall in love. Our family's magic is awakened when we meet our soulmate. My sister has such great instincts when it comes to matchmaking. Maybe it wasn't an accident that she sent you here after all. Did you bring the cookbook down with you?"

Devon's legs felt like lead weights as she walked over to the cupboard where she'd left the cookbook. When she'd first arrived in the kitchen this morning, she'd made a space between the cooking pots and pans on the cupboard shelves. "I put it on the shelf so I wouldn't get it dirty while I was baking." She hesitated. "That can't be. The cookbook is missing."

"Not missing. Stolen."

Chapter Eleven

Graham regretted how he had left things with Devon. He had not been truthful with her when he said he'd never seen her before. But admitting the truth might place her in more danger, and that he would not do.

The shadows in the forest below the castle elongated like the hands of ghosts reaching out for their next victim. The prearranged meeting place had all the earmarks of an ambush. Graham rested his hand on the hilt of his sword as he approached the beech trees, their bone-like branches stretched toward the ebony night sky, enhancing his sense of foreboding. His mother always said he had a keen sense of survival. He prayed she was right.

"Did you find it?"

Graham recognized the stone-cold voice. Lord Basil had once been Graham's employer, then his benefactor. Now the man was his enemy.

"The woman who works in the kitchen is not the one you seek," Graham lied. He had dodged Lord Basil's question, stalling for time and information.

Lord Basil stepped out of the shadows. With his blond hair, blue eyes, and snow-white tunic, Lord Basil was the image of a fabled knight of the Round Table. Beneath the handsome exterior beat a black heart. "My spies say the woman's name is Devon, and she has one blue eye and one green. She has to be the one."

"Your spies also told you that the woman you were looking for was in the twilight years of her life, not the bloom of youth and beauty."

Lord Basil paced under the canopy of trees. Graham knew his best option was delay and distraction. Lord Basil kept his mother prisoner, and Graham had vowed to rescue her. He waited for Lord Basil's response. Waiting was not one of Graham's strengths. He was a man of action, not patience. But he must exercise patience. The safety of his mother and of Devon hung in the balance. If he saved one, he would lose the other. That was not an option. He must save both.

Lord Basil spun around, naked evil shining in his eyes. "The young woman called Devon, with one blue eye and one green, must be related to the older woman. You will force Devon to tell you the location of the cookbook."

"Devon is a servant in the Queen's kitchen and has access to many cookbooks. She will not understand which one we need. What is so special about this cookbook that you would risk threatening my mother, thus assuring my revenge if she is harmed?"

Lord Basil pressed his thin lips together and hesitated as though weighing how much he wanted to share. "All you need to know is that I have ordered you to bring me the cookbook, and this woman, in exchange for your mother's freedom."

Graham gripped the hilt of his sword tighter. "I will not proceed until you answer my question. What is the importance of this cookbook?"

"Fine," Lord Basil ground out. "The cookbook has the power to control time."

Graham kept his expression devoid of emotion, a

lesson he had learned early in life. Hidden under Graham's tunic, he felt the weight of the cookbook press against him as though it had a life of its own and recognized the danger. Graham knew Lord Basil was one of John Dee's apprentices and both were involved in the dark occult. In their hands, the cookbook would be a formidable weapon. Graham could not allow that to happen.

"You speak of sorcery," Graham said. "Are you sure this is the path you wish to tread?"

"Spare me the righteous sermon. Your mother is a witch, and I know you are familiar with the arts. Do not worry about sorcery. Worry about bringing me the cookbook and the woman. If they are not in my possession by Christmas, your mother will die."

Chapter Twelve

Not missing. Stolen.

The words Charlotte had spoken last night haunted Devon as she perched on a stool near the kitchen hearth. She'd kept the fire burning through the night more for comfort than heat. She was so confused, and she needed answers. Why had it taken traveling to the sixteenth century for her powers to appear? Under the circumstances, the wood fire, with its subtle incense aroma, seemed fitting. That same aroma had been present in the shop where she'd found the cookbook.

Dawn on Christmas Day was approaching, and she was no closer to finding her cookbook than when she'd begun her search. Feeling defeated, she gazed toward the fire until her vision blurred. Since arriving here, she'd taken great care of the cookbook because of its connection to her grandmother and her life in the twenty-first century. Then she had learned it might have more than sentimental value. It had magical properties, and according to Charlotte there was the possibility that it held the power to send her back home. The real question was whether or not she wanted to return. Her powers had been released in the sixteenth century. Would they disappear in the twenty-first? And what about Graham?

Her constant state of limbo threatened to overwhelm her. She squeezed her eyes shut to keep it at bay and slid off the stool. The gingerbread castle stood in all its glory on a worktable against the wall. The benefit of a sleepless night meant she had been able to finish the structure. There were towers, a gatehouse, drawbridge, and a mote made from glass-like sugar. Interior walls were painted with tapestry-like scenes of life in Elizabethan times and Charlotte's collection of gingerbread nobles and knights were arranged in the ballroom.

She, Charlotte, and Graham, had created a fantasy castle that would have enchanted Cinderella and her Prince Charming. The centerpiece was breathtaking and hopefully would be a hit with the Queen and her court. Only a few days ago the Queen's approval had been Devon's sole concern.

It seemed a lifetime ago. With her cookbook missing, a more pressing problem took center stage. The fairies inside the gingerbread walls were still animated. Devon had no idea how to make them stop dancing. Of course, she hadn't a clue how she'd animated them in the first place or how she would explain them to the Queen without sounding like a sorceress. Was the missing cookbook connected to her newfound powers?

Devon pressed the heel of her hand against her forehead. All this hypothetical thinking was making her dizzy. Everything seemed to circle back to the cookbook. She draped the gingerbread castle with a cloth and a sigh. "What am I going to do?" she said to herself as Charlotte entered the kitchen from the back door.

Charlotte set down a basket of freshly cut holly by the hearth. She had changed her hair style. Instead of arranging it in a tight circle of braids on top of her head, she'd allowed a few curls to frame her face and had secured her long white hair with a red ribbon at the base of her neck. Devon was speechless at Charlotte's transformation. Her grand-aunt looked years younger.

"I think the holly would look nice over the fireplace mantel. Don't you agree?"

Devon gave a quick nod, too stunned by Charlotte's transformation to point out that the hearth in the kitchen didn't have a mantel. "Charlotte, you look lovely this morning. Are you wearing lipstick?"

Charlotte touched her mouth. "A little rouge is all. Well, well, what do we have here?" She lifted a corner of the cloth covering the gingerbread castle. "This is a work of art and your fairies a lively bunch. They are all dressed like noblewomen, in red and gold gowns. You'd have thought they'd have tired of dancing by now. Could you ask them to help us with the baking? It's Christmas Day, and the Queen sent Mr. Lum an order for more plates and goblets made from rose-tinted sugar."

Devon folded her arms across her chest. Why did her grand-aunt seem changed and taking this predicament so lightly? "Dancing fairies are not a joking matter."

"Who said I was joking?"

"Charlotte, I can't control the fairies. Even if I could, the last thing I'd do would be to ask them to help us in the kitchen. We'd be thrown in the tower and accused of witchcraft faster than you could say 'chocolate torte.' I'm not sure how I animated them in the first place."

Charlotte took Devon's hands in hers. "I admit I was joking a little about the fairies before. Think back. Did you do or say anything right before the fairies sprang to life? For example, in the movie remake of the TV series *Bewitched*, the actress Nicole Kidman, who played the character Samantha, twitched her nose when she performed magic. My sister clapped her hands—or did she wave them? I can never remember."

Devon understood the direction of Charlotte's comments. "My mother snaps her fingers, and I've heard her use the expression, 'Let's see,' but I never thought they were magical words."

"Perhaps not, although all words are powerful." Charlotte paused. "Both your mother and grandmother use their hands. That can't be a coincidence." Charlotte focused on the gingerbread castle. "Why don't you try to ask the fairies to take a nap? You can begin with how my sister and your mother initiated their magic."

Devon drew in a deep breath, while visualizing the fairies falling into a restful sleep. She snapped her fingers. Nothing. Except she could have sworn that the fairies increased the tempo of the dance just to show off. She tried again, this time using the words, "Let's see." The fairies kept dancing, and one wearing a red gown had the audacity to wink and blow a kiss. Devon narrowed her gaze at the fairy and clapped like she'd seen her grandmother do countless times. The fairies burst out laughing.

She tilted her head back in frustration. "This isn't working. The fairies are mocking me, and the one in the red dress is rolling her eyes."

Charlotte covered the gingerbread castle and pressed her finger to her mouth. "Don't say another word. The cooks are arriving."

Conversation echoed in the corridor outside the kitchen and grew louder as the doors opened and a flood of people walked in ready for work. Mr. Lum wore a new embroidered waistcoat and had trimmed his hair and beard. The tone of his voice seemed gentle as he directed people to their tasks. When he finished, he cast Charlotte a shy smile.

Charlotte blushed, grabbed a sack of flour from the floor, and set it on the worktable as she concentrated on measuring flour into a bowl.

Devon looked between Mr. Lum and Charlotte. Devon didn't have to be a matchmaker or a reader of romance novels to recognize budding love when she saw it. She smiled and nudged Charlotte's shoulder. "So? You and Mr. Lum?"

"Mr. Lum is a most irritating man." Charlotte's cheeks turned a deeper rose pink. "He is also sweet when he wants to be."

"Hold on. Were you with him last night? Is that the reason you left the cryptic note on our nightstand? The one that read, 'Be back soon'?"

Charlotte's blush deepened as she added another cup of flour. "I am sure I have no idea what you are talking about. I was working late in the kitchen."

Devon chuckled. "Nice try. I was in the kitchen all night looking for my cookbook. You like him. Admit it. I gather he's not the ogre we thought."

Charlotte smiled as she measured more flour. "Not an ogre at all. In fact, he is rather robust in bed—if you know what I mean?"

Devon let out with a short laugh, drawing curious glances from the kitchen staff and a raised eyebrow from Mr. Lum. "I'm happy for you. but you are my grand-aunt and the less detail the better. Agreed?"

"Agreed."

Devon retrieved from the cupboard the metal molds she used to make sugar glass plates, placing them on the worktable in a row. She was behaving just like Charlotte, going about their duties in the kitchen instead of trying to find the missing cookbook. "We should talk about the cookbook."

Charlotte nodded. "Do you have any idea who might have stolen it?"

The whole idea someone had stolen something that important to her was disturbing. "I haven't a clue who stole my cookbook. There were so many people in and out of the kitchen yesterday. It could be anyone."

"Ah," was Charlotte's only response as she measured another cup of flour into the bowl. "Do you think it might have been Sir Graham?"

Devon felt as though her heart had stopped beating. Why had Charlotte accused Graham? Devon stood frozen at the table while activity buzzed around her. The ovens were fed wood, while crowded workstations were full of men and women preparing dough for tarts, pies, and bread. On a normal day, the sound of an active kitchen was soothing. Now the sounds were deafening and grated on her nerves. She wanted to be alone to sort out Charlotte's disturbing accusation against Graham.

She relived the moments she'd shared with Graham, their kiss, their collaboration on the gingerbread house, the moment when she realized she cared for him... She shook her head. And then when she suspected he could be lying about seeing her before. What possible reason would he have had to steal the cookbook?

Someone dropped a skillet on the stone floor, and she flinched.

"Devon. Are you okay?"

"No, I am not...okay. You accused Graham of stealing. How could you suggest such a thing? Besides, you are the one who said Graham was responsible for the sudden awakening of my gifts."

Charlotte glanced over her shoulder to make sure no one was listening to their conversation. "I stand by what I said, but it was something Mr. Lum mentioned regarding Lord Basil that started me thinking. Mr. Lum overheard him mention that he was looking for a cookbook, and I know Sir Graham works for him. It can't be a coincidence."

"Grandmother said there's no such thing as a coincidence."

"Exactly. And you are coming into your powers. Most in our family have limited and very targeted gifts. Animation is an advanced skill. I want to believe Sir Graham's appearance has nothing to do with Lord Basil." As though distracted, she added more flour. "But what if it is not?"

The revelation about Lord Basil added another layer to Devon's confusion and panic. She'd never told Charlotte she'd seen a knight on horseback before she'd traveled back in time and, more importantly, that she suspected Graham might be the knight. She wanted to believe Graham was just as he appeared—a kind man with whom she'd felt a deep and instant connection. What if his appearance wasn't an accident?

She sorted the metal molds for the glass plates according to size, from smaller to larger. "There's something I need to tell you."

As though deep in thought, Charlotte didn't look up. She kept measuring flour into the bowl like a mechanical robot on an assembly line.

Devon waved her hand to get Charlotte's attention. "Stop. Why do you need so much flour? It looks like you're preparing to build a giant flour monster."

Without warning, the flour in Charlotte's bowl expanded and mushroomed over the sides, growing in volume like a balloon filling with helium. It doubled in size, then tripled, then tripled again.

Charlotte stepped back with a pleased expression. "Very impressive."

Devon looked at her hands and the growing flour balloon. Had she caused the flour to expand?

Charlotte nudged her and mouthed the words, "Make it stop."

Devon hesitated, not understanding what Charlotte meant. When Charlotte repeated her request, it felt to Devon as though a light had been turned on, and she realized exactly what to do. She waved her hands in the direction of the flour balloon again, and whispered, "Stop!"

The balloon burst like it had been pricked with a pin and exploded, showering Devon and Charlotte in a dusting of flour.

The noise in the kitchens paused as though someone had turned on the simmer button. Charlotte wiped flour from her face and apron. Suppressing a smile, she whispered, "Nicely done." She then raised her voice to include everyone in the kitchen. "It was an accident," she said licking flour from her lips and held up the sack of flour. "My apologies. I mishandled the sack, and it spilled everywhere."

Mr. Lum strolled over to Charlotte; his gaze focused on her mouth. His voice softened. "All right, then. Clean up the flour. Everyone back to work. Today is Christmas, and there is much to do to prepare for the evening meal and the Queen's After Party. A lord and his retinue arrived late last night with more demands than a dozen nobles put together." When the kitchen staff had resumed working, his glance settled once again on Charlotte, and the corners of his mouth lifted in a smile. "Might I have a word with you, Charlotte?"

Charlotte's cheeks under the coating of flour turned pink like a schoolgirl with her first crush. She hesitated long enough to give Devon a smile and a nod, then followed Mr. Lum into the corridor.

Devon went about the business of cleaning up the flour. The strange incident with the exploding flour replayed in her thoughts. She knew exactly what had happened. Charlotte had used the flour to provoke Devon to use magic, and it had worked. She'd waved her hand, directed her thoughts toward the flour, and created a giant balloon. Could it have been that simple?

She scooped the flour from the worktable into the bowl and scanned the kitchen. Mr. Lum and Charlotte were still in the corridor, and the kitchen staff was busy preparing desserts for tonight's Christmas celebration. While everyone was occupied, Devon decided to try her newfound theory on how to use her magic.

She moved around toward the back of the gingerbread castle and lifted a corner of the cloth near the dancing fairies. She crouched down low, waved her hand, and whispered. "Fairies. Go to sleep."

Instantly, the fairies stopped dancing and closed their eyes.

"What are you doing behind the gingerbread castle?" Graham's voice loomed over her, dark and rich like hot fudge.

She rose so fast she turned into his arms and into a smile that heated the air and threated to banish all rational thoughts from her head. She felt as light as the flour balloon as she gazed into his eyes.

Then Charlotte's comment that Graham might have been the thief crashed her back down to earth. Why had Charlotte put the thought in her mind? And, of course, there was the whole question of whether he was or wasn't the knight she'd seen before she'd time traveled…

Her hand was still pressed against his chest, and she told herself it was there to keep her from losing her balance. She snatched it to her side and tore her gaze from his. "I have to ask you a question. More than one, actually."

Chapter Thirteen

The kitchen hummed with activity as Devon reached for her shawl. A short time ago she had asked Graham to meet her outside in the walled vegetable garden. Mr. Lum and Charlotte had returned from their conversation in the corridor, both rosy checked and flushed as though they had shared a kiss. Charlotte said she'd cover for Devon's absence, but it didn't look like it would be a problem. Mr. Lum was talking to an agitated nobleman, whose back was turned toward Devon. The man wore a large starched white ruff around his neck, a crimson doublet, purple-and-gold-striped hose, and strutted like a peacock, demanding attention as if he were the king of the castle.

Keeping her head down to avoid conversation, she headed along the corridor that led to the garden and pushed open the door. A light powder-like snow covered rows of beets, carrots, onions, and potatoes, allowing only the green and berry-colored foliage to peek through. Snow turned to sleet, and like a soldier preparing for battle, Devon swept the shawl over her shoulders as though it were armor.

She saw Graham waiting for her at the entrance to the garden, and as soon as they stepped outside, he'd headed over to the ivy-covered stone wall where a section had been dedicated to a lone English walnut tree. He reached past the silvery gray bark into the dark green leaves. The leaves fluttered, and there was a flash of red, as though he had released something into the heart of the branches.

Graham had seemed a little on edge when he left the kitchen, but looked calmer now, which only made her more agitated. Why should he look relaxed when she was a jumble of nerves?

Was Charlotte correct? Had Graham stolen the cookbook? Devon didn't want to believe Charlotte's suspicions—that came as the response from her heart. And if he had, it meant everything that had passed between them was built on lies. He might not be the chivalrous knight she'd thought him to be.

How could he have known the cookbook held magical powers, when she'd only learned its secrets recently? If the book hadn't zapped her fingers when she touched it, she might never have put it together. Most people she knew only needed one or two clues to solve a puzzle. She required animated gingerbread men, fairies, and exploding flour balloons.

Graham had turned away from the walnut tree and walked toward her as though in slow motion, each step causing her pulse to race faster. Had he grown taller? His gaze scanned hers, and the color of his eyes reminded her of heated caramel. Her attraction to him warred with reason. There was more to him than met the eye. Somehow, he and the cookbook were connected.

He handed her a walnut he had shelled. "I missed you." His words were warm and sounded sincere.

The handful of shelled walnuts seemed more than a peace offering. Walnuts were part of legends and fairytales, like the story "The Iron Stove" by the Brothers Grimm. In the story, a princess received three walnuts with the promise they would help her win the heart of a handsome prince. When she opened the walnut, she discovered a dress made from spun gold. Devon closed her fingers around the shelled pieces and pressed her lips together as she fought against saying she had missed him too.

"You are covered in flour, and you look like you are cold."

He had made a normal comment, and on any other day, she'd have thought of an equally normal response. Today was not one of those days.

Shivering, she tightened her hold on the shawl, the walnut pieces biting into the palm of her hand. The sleet mixed with the flour to form a clumpy mess in her hair. Of all days to forget her head covering, she'd picked today. To add insult to injury, Graham looked yummy and kissable. She wanted to kill him.

"Yes, I'm freezing." The cold and chattering teeth made her words slur. It was not at all the forceful tone she had hoped for. "Thank you, Sir Obvious." She pushed past the cold and her annoyance and went straight to the point. "Charlotte believes you stole my grandmother's cookbook. Did you?" She braced for his denial and more lies.

"I had a good reason." He reached toward her and tried to put his arm around her shoulders. "You are cold," he repeated. "Let us go inside where it is warmer."

She jerked his hand away. "I'm just fine. Do not do the Chivalrous Knight thing you do. Give it back."

"I cannot."

His words triggered dormant emotions, and her eyes brimmed with tears she'd kept at bay since she'd arrived. From the day she traveled back in time, she had fought against mounting anger toward her grandmother for her predicament. If it hadn't been for Charlotte, Devon knew she wouldn't have made it. But through it all, Devon had made the most of living without indoor plumbing, hot showers, and electricity. It was not until she learned the cookbook could send her back home that she'd let her guard down and started to hope. Then, almost in the same breath, she'd met Graham. More hope. More shattered dreams.

Hot tears spilled down her cheeks, and she swiped them away. "What do you mean you can't return the cookbook? I want it back. Now!"

The faraway sound of men's shouts drifted over the frosted gardens. Inside the castle, muffled running, as heavy boots met stone floors. The clink of armor echoed down the corridors and headed in the direction of the kitchens.

Graham glanced over his shoulder in the direction of the sound, his voice distracted. "You left it out in the open on the cupboard shelf where someone might find it."

"Are you trying to tell me you stole my cookbook to keep it safe?" She hated the direction of their argument. She'd heard some chefs, protective of their recipes and fearing unscrupulous people intent on stealing them to bolster their careers, locked their cookbooks in a safe. She knew Graham hadn't stolen her cookbook because he thought someone wanted her recipe for gingerbread.

Worried lines cut deep tracks in his forehead as he glanced over his shoulder again. "We should move away out of sight." He motioned her over to the side of the stonewall and an iron gate hidden behind a canopy of trees. He raked the wet hair back from his forehead as his eyes held her in a haunted gaze. "There is someone searching for you and your cookbook who believes it is more than recipes. I was uncertain if you had it until…"

"…until we kissed," she finished, as a lump formed in her throat. She remembered the kiss. No one had ever kissed her the way Graham had, and she knew in her heart no one ever would. The kiss spoke of love and forever after.

He shook his head. "Not our kiss, although it changed me, and my path. Ultimately it was what you said that confirmed my suspicions that I had found what was lost. I was to find a woman with one blue eye and one green who was in possession of a cookbook with an etching in gold of two crossed spoons on the cover. Even when I saw the cookbook on the kitchen shelf, I was not sure until you told me about the knight you had seen who had spoken to you in your thoughts." He hesitated. "You are angry with me, and you have good reason. I lied when I said I had never seen you before. Your question took me by surprise. I had seen you too…in a dream."

"Liar." She'd said the word softly, but the word screamed so loud in her head she'd barely heard what had come next. When her ears stopped ringing from the thought of his betrayal of trust, she remembered what he'd said about seeing her in a dream. It made no sense. She'd been wide awake when she'd seen him. She had been returning from the bookstore with the cookbook and had seen him on the grounds of the Dundees' estate where her family was catering the wedding.

He was holding back. She could see it in the tension around his eyes. Weighing the risk of saying what might be considered in the realm of magic, she relied on the adage "nothing ventured, nothing gained."

She was tired of being afraid. "I wasn't dreaming when I saw you." She held her breath, bracing for him to call her a witch.

Muffled shouts grew louder, and the same nobleman she'd seen talking to Mr. Lum in the kitchen earlier appeared framed in the garden's entrance. The man was too far away to see his face. His words, however, rang out loud and clear, like the tolling of a bell.

"Find the woman with one blue eye and one green," he shouted, "and bring her to me."

Graham pulled Devon behind him, opened the gate, and took her hand. "There is more I need to tell you, and most you will not like. For now, the more pressing matter is escape."

Chapter Fourteen

Graham knew the next few hours would determine who lived and who died. The gray sky of dusk and building storm clouds cast long shadows, aiding escape. Taking Devon's hand in his, he guided her through the wall's iron gate, in the direction of the river that meandered alongside the castle.

Devon had a right to be angry with him. He rationalized he had stolen her cookbook to keep it safe. A partial truth. He knew it was only a matter of time before Lord Basil found the cookbook, and he did not want him to find it with Devon. He should have told her the whole truth from the beginning. His mother was a witch, and he knew she was involved but as yet did not know how this would play out. How could he explain it to Devon when he did not understand it all himself?

What he did know was that Devon had become important to him, and he vowed to keep her safe. And the first order of business was to find her a place to hide.

He tightened her hand in his, and together they raced across a footbridge. The bridge was constructed over the water passageway that ran beneath the castle and was used to transport supplies. He was hoping this underground passageway would be the last place Lord Basil and his men would look.

He broke the lock on the gate guarding the passageway. A stone dock hugged one side, allowing the river to flow freely on the other. Keeping to the dock side, Graham and Devon entered. The passageway had been constructed over a fast-moving stream that joined a river bordering the town. Swollen from rain, the stream ran parallel to the stone dock as gusts of wind whipped the water into stiff, cream-like peaks. With Devon beside him, he slowed his pace as he reached the dock where a few wooden rowboats were moored.

Feral cats, ranging in shade from cream to ginger to chocolate brown, patrolled the dock in the passageway in search of rodents. Startled, they crouched low, eyeing the human intrusion. One by one they flowed into the shadows or in the direction of oak barrels stacked near a winding stone stairway. A few held back and hissed their objections before following their comrades.

It was as though the cats were berating him for not foreseeing Lord Basil's next move. Graham was furious with himself.

But Graham had believed he had more time. Somehow Lord Basil had learned a woman with one blue eye and one green worked in the kitchen. Graham should have foreseen this turn of events. Lord Basil never relied on one source for information once he learned the probable location of the item he sought. Once discovered, he had let loose an army of spies for confirmation.

Graham paused by the most seaworthy-looking of the rowboats that bobbed in the stream as a plan formed. It would take time for Lord Basil to search the castle for Devon. Graham would use that time to row Devon to safety. He knew someone in town he could trust who would keep her safe. Then he would return and offer the cookbook in exchange for his mother's freedom.

His decision made, he motioned toward Devon. "Get into the boat. We are going into town." He winced. His words had come out more harshly than he had intended.

Her brows pulled together in a frown as she stepped away from him. She had slipped her hand from his and the absence of her touch made the world a colder place. "I will not get in the leaky old boat until you explain to me what is going on. Why is that peacock of a man looking for me? Does it have to do with the cookbook?" Her eyes narrowed. "The cookbook you stole from me."

"I told you. I stole it to keep it safe."

"So you keep saying. I need to know why."

She had grasped the danger and the cause. Her intelligence and calm only made him care for her more, and he knew in that moment he would protect her with his last breath. She had also described Lord Basil as a peacock. The description fit. Lord Basil was all about appearances. "You deserve to know it all, and you are correct. We do not have much time. I promise I will tell you along our journey to town."

She raised her chin. "I'm not moving a muscle. Tell me now."

He could lie to her—again. Pretend he knew nothing of the world of magic. Pretend he had not seen her expand flour into a white globe or bring gingerbread fairies to life. In the vegetable garden, after he had released the fairy in the red dress into the walnut tree, he had wanted to tell Devon everything. About how his mother had abandoned him as a babe to a childless couple who had loved him as though he were their own. After they died, he had searched for his birth mother, found her, and had regretted it ever since. About how, after falling in love with Devon, he did not want the life of an adventurer—he wanted only her.

He took in a deep breath, releasing it slowly and wishing he could release his past as easily. He would start with where he believed this had begun. "My mother is a powerful witch, and I feel her hand in this. Have, in fact, for some time."

He allowed his statement to stand on its own as he regarded her reactions. She performed magic, but to declare oneself a witch was to invite danger. One of the Queen's advisors, a man by the name of John Dee, was into the dark arts but wisely refused to accept the title of wizard or sorcerer.

When Devon did not respond, he continued. "My mother is being imprisoned by the man in the garden you called a peacock. His name is Lord Basil, and he sent me to find you and your cookbook in exchange for my mother's freedom. He believes it has the power to control time." Graham knew what he said sounded strange to some, but he was talking to a person who had made gingerbread fairies come to life.

She shuddered and glanced at the shelled walnuts she still held in her hand. "Lord Basil is correct. The cookbook does control time, that's why I'm here, but I'm really not sure how it works." Wide-eyed, she lifted her gaze to his. "I understand now why you needed the cookbook."

He prayed he was worthy of the trust he saw in their depths. "I just told you my mother is a witch. You said you saw me in your time and that I talked to you in your thoughts. My mother's doing, no doubt. You also have magic. You made gingerbread fairies come to life. I released one into the walnut tree in the garden, by the way. She was not happy in the kitchen. So, traveling to the future no longer seems fantastical to me."

Devon's smile reached her eyes. "Was the fairy you released wearing a red dress?" With his nod, she laughed. "I thought she was missing. I'm glad."

Although she had not said the words, he was positive she had forgiven him for taking her cookbook. He recognized it in the gentle tone of her voice and the warmth of her gaze. Her forgiveness was a greater miracle to him than all the magic he had seen his mother perform.

"I will not let Lord Basil harm you," he blurted. "I cannot. I will take you to safety. I shall make up a story that you drowned, and then offer him the cookbook in exchange for my mother. If Lord Basil captures you, he will not kill you right away. He will force you, by any means necessary, to teach him the magic secrets of the cookbook and how it controls time. Please get into the boat."

She glanced at the walnuts again, and a smile flickered over her lips like sunlight over a mountain lake. "All Lord Basil knows is that the person he is looking for has one blue eye and one green. I'm just a servant among hundreds of servants in the castle. He's looking for someone dressed in shapeless, drab-brown clothes." She popped one of the shelled walnuts into her mouth. "I have a better idea than running away. But we are going to need to find a fairy godmother."

Chapter Fifteen

Shadows deepened in the underground passageway beneath the castle, seeping into Devon's bones as the sun set and slipped from sight. Twin torches hung on metal sconces, giving off a miserly glow as gentle waves lapped against the boats, rocking them back and forth. The only other sounds were the clowder of multi-colored cats meowing as they circled a supply of beer barrels that had been unloaded and stacked on the dock. She stood beside Graham in silence, searching for something to say.

He was focused on the frozen chunks of ice floating in the water as though he could melt them with his gaze. She'd told him of her plan, and with Charlette's help, she'd switch the cookbooks, instead of running away. Graham dismissed the idea as doomed to fail, and his slow burn of disapproval had grown. Obviously, he wasn't accustomed to a woman challenging his advice. She got it. He wanted to keep her safe. But she'd seen this movie storyline before.

She and Graham would climb into one of the docked wooden boats. They would row over water so cold that ice, the size of commercial cookie sheets, might break through the hull, capsizing their boat. Then, if they weren't ambushed, or the boat didn't sink, drowning them, and if they survived hyperthermia and reached the shore, Graham planned to turn her over to a complete stranger. Maybe he'd come back for her. More likely he would die. Then what? No, thank you. Concern over how to open a stalled conversation diplomatically evaporated.

"I'm not getting into that boat." She punctuated each word with a stamp of her foot. "Why won't you reconsider my plan?"

His scowl deepened, his eyes so dark they looked as black as coal. "You are not safe here." He said it as though that ended the discussion.

She faced him with a scowl of her own. "What makes you sure I'll be safe in town if you are dead?"

"I am not going to die."

She choked back a laugh. "Said by every warrior-type since the dawn of history right before he or she went into battle—and died. Look. I understand you feel this is some sort of 'me Tarzan, you Jane' scenario, where you keep the little woman hidden and go off and defeat an army singlehandedly. If Lord Basil is everything you say he is, he will not stop until he finds me."

Graham shrugged his shoulders. "I do not know who Tarzan and Jane are, but perhaps you are right. I shall have to kill Lord Basil."

She pressed her lips together, feeling the urge to pummel Graham with one of the boat's oars. Typical. The man wasn't listening. "Oh, really? I estimate Lord Basil brought about twenty men with him."

"Closer to fifty."

"My mistake. Of course, he brought fifty well-trained, well-armed men. What was I thinking? Let me guess. Your plan is to kill them and Lord Basil. You are as adorable as the actor Keanu Reeves, but you are not John Wick."

"Who?"

"Not important." She was worried and frustrated with him and couldn't seem to break through his tough macho hide. He was going to get himself killed, and she refused to stand by and watch.

Graham lifted his gaze toward the entrance. "I smell smoke."

"If you are implying I'm smoking mad, you are…"

He shook his head and pointed to the entrance, as he reached for her hand and drew her from the edge of the dock. "I thought we would have more time."

She followed his gaze, expecting a cloak of darkness. Instead, sparks of light danced in the shifting winds like restless fireflies on a summer night. The low murmuring of men's voices and clanking armor intruded. Scarlet and amber flames from a dozen or more torches filled the entrance. She knew if they attempted to escape by boat now, they would be seen and captured.

She pulled her shawl closer around her shoulders. "Maybe they won't come in here."

"We cannot take the chance," Graham said. "We have to hide."

"What about the stairs?"

"Too far away. We will be seen if we run in that direction. Our only chance is to hide and hope they pass us by."

Devon scrambled with Graham behind the pyramid of beer barrels.

No sooner had they ducked out of sight than the soldiers advanced forward. Shadows from their torches climbed the walls as though helping the soldiers search. Devon pressed against Graham in the cramped space, feeling his heart beat in unison with hers. What would happen if the soldiers found her? All the stories she'd heard about the violence in this century scrolled through her thoughts. She shook until her teeth chattered.

He pulled her closer. "I will not let them harm you."

Graham had spoken those words before, and she knew he meant them, but they were outnumbered. She pressed her lips together. All she could do was nod. How could he keep such a promise?

A roar of light burst and brought with it the brightness of the sun and a loud exchange of conversation. The half dozen soldiers were a chatty bunch. They debated how best to search the castle and grounds and the prediction they'd find the girl with one blue and one green eye in time to enjoy the food and entertainment of the local tavern in town tonight.

Wedged behind a tower of oak barrels, Devon couldn't see what was happening on the other side. She lowered her voice to a whisper. "What are they doing?"

"They are burning the boats," Graham said in a low, flat tone, his expression drawn and hard. "Knowing Lord Basil's men as I do, their next step will be to search the area. Our only chance is to create a diversion. How strong is your magic?"

"Not very. My family calls what we do 'kitchen magic.' Our gifts involve food and its ingredients." She pulled up straighter. "Wait. I have an idea. Although beer is technically a beverage, it contains water, hops, barley, and yeast, and what yeast loves to do best is expand."

Imagining the beer in the barrels expanding, she waved her hand and whispered, "Let's see."

The barrels before her rocked back and forth as gently as the boats had moments before. Beer inside the barrels splashed and the wood creaked as the liquid expanded.

Devon waved her hand toward the other barrels, and like the first ones, they started to groan and shake and rattle against each other. Beer inside expanded, testing the metal bands, holding the staves in place.

In the dock area, one of the soldiers shouted, "Did you hear something?"

"Get ready to run," Devon waved her hand again for good measure. The whole idea of using magic was new and she didn't know how much spell casting was too much or just enough.

The barrel closest to her rocked violently, destabilizing the pyramid. The lids on the barrels on top of the pyramid popped off like Champagne corks, shooting beer into the air. Beer and foam rained down, drenching them to the skin.

Graham pulled Devon out of the way and shielded her as barrels toppled down and metal bands snapped. Barrels still intact rolled in all directions, scattering soldiers on the dock. Some jumped into the water, still holding their torches, while others ran out of the passageway, and a few remained and stood nearby too stunned to move.

"Halt," the soldier on the dock shouted as he turned toward Devon and Graham. He held the torch he carried higher. "Show yourself."

"It is Sir Graham," his comrade with an eyepatch said. "What are you doing here?" The soldier narrowed his one good eye. "If this is the woman Lord Basil seeks, turn her over."

Graham unsheathed his sword. "I will not."

"You are making a mistake," the soldier holding the torch said.

"If you challenge me, it will be you who is making

the mistake."

The man with the torch nodded toward his one-eyed comrade to move toward Devon. The man tossed his torch aside and drew his sword. "Sir Graham, are you as good as they say?"

Graham smiled. "Better." He turned toward Devon. "I will hold them off. "Run for the stairs."

He was asking her to leave him alone to fend off the attack. She wouldn't. She looked around for anything she could use as a weapon against the unarmed, one-eyed soldier, who moved in her direction.

She reached for one of the oak staves that had come loose and gripped it like a baseball bat. When the man with the eyepatch was close enough, she swung for his head and heard a cracking sound. He stumbled back into the broken barrels, crumpled into the pile, and lost consciousness.

Still holding the stave, she glanced toward Graham and the battle he waged.

One of the soldiers, who had jumped into the water when the barrels were exploding, pulled himself onto the dock, drew his sword, and joined the attack on Graham.

The sound of metal-on-metal cut through the air as swords clashed. For now, Graham was holding his own, but if reinforcements arrived, that would change. This was not a movie—this was real life. Graham's idea to use the stairs to escape was a good one, except the entrance was blocked by the debris from the exploding barrels. If she could clear the entrance, they might have a chance. Keeping hold of her makeshift weapon, she headed for the staircase to pull debris out of the way.

From the corner of her eye she saw Graham launch a counterattack on his opponents and drive them to the water's edge. He sidestepped the shorter of the two and knocked him unconscious with the hilt of his sword, then turned his attention on the man who remained. When the man pointed his sword toward Graham and lunged, Graham redirected the attack with his blade and pushed the soldier's sword away with such force it flew from the soldier's grip and into the water. Attempting to reach for his blade, the soldier lost his balance and splashed into the water.

Graham turned on his heels and raced toward Devon, helping her to clear the stairwell's door of the remaining debris. As the sound of reinforcements filled the passageway, Graham shut the door behind them and bolted it. "This will not hold them for long."

"Come. I know where we can hide."

Chapter Sixteen

Devon shivered as she led Graham through a labyrinth of passageways between the castle walls. He was close behind her, matching his pace with hers. His presence was reassuring, as was the occasional scrape of his sword against the stone walls of the narrow passageway. He was a man of his word, had protected her against Lord Basil's men, and in so doing, had assured that Lord Basil would know Graham would protect Devon with his life.

She was in love with Graham. In truth, she had been falling in love with him from the moment he'd come to Bran's rescue. Why had it taken her traveling back in time to discover a man she could love with her whole heart?

Heart pounding, she brushed away sticky spider webs from her face and sidestepped to avoid others. She was drenched to the skin in beer and no doubt smelled like a brewery. She and Graham had almost been captured, and yes, her magic had produced a distraction, but she'd underestimated the power of the spell she'd cast. They could have been crushed under the exploding beer barrels. She needed to figure out a way to control her magic, and fast. But what overlay all the problems they faced was knowing they belonged together, and that gave her hope.

She reached a crossroads in the passageway and

motioned for Graham to follow her on the one that continued to climb. Charlotte had told her stories of people who had been lost for hours, days, and sometimes longer. Did she hear soldier's footsteps below, or was it the thundering sound of blood pumping though her veins?

Learning how to navigate the secret passageways was one of the first things Charlotte had taught her, as well as identifying marks on the different doors and where they would lead. Charlotte had also told her the place for them to meet if either of them were in trouble. The passageway widened, and on Devon's right was a wood panel door with a small Scottish Thistle carved into the center panel. Devon pressed down on the iron lever and opened the door a fraction of an inch, peering inside the room at the familiar surroundings.

The room was used to store the Queen's gowns and those of her ladies in waiting. Dresses and cloaks in jeweled tones—ruby red, sapphire blue, emerald green, and golden amber—hung on clothes racks. Large wardrobes lined two of the walls and were packed with more clothes, hats, and accessories. It was not unlike the backstage of a theatre where actors changed into costumes for the parts they played. The thought gave Devon an idea.

"The room is empty. Follow me."

Graham ducked under the entrance. "You were fearless against the soldier who attacked you." There was respect in the tone of his voice, and something more intimate.

"Thank you. You were pretty fierce yourself."

"I had to be. I did not want the soldiers to harm you. You are important to me."

She warmed under his words, resting her hand on his arm, feeling his muscles flex beneath her touch. "You are important to me as well."

"How can that be? I am…"

"You are wonderful. My own personal knight in shining armor. But as much as I'd like to pursue this line of thinking, we need to develop a plan to save your mother without having to turn over the cookbook to Lord Basil."

"I would very much like to hear this plan of yours," he said as he glanced around the room.

"It's in the beginning stages. I wish I had a better handle on my magic, though. I might be able to animate gingerbread fairies and cause flour to expand, but as you witnessed with the wine barrels, my magic is unstable, and I haven't a clue how the cookbook's magic works when it comes to time travel."

"Were you afraid when you first realized you had traveled back in time? I have traveled and seen all manner of strange wonders, and not all experiences were positive."

She blew on her hands to warm them. "It was scary at first, but Charlotte was here to help me, and because I studied history, I at least knew what to expect. My biggest concern was saying or doing something that might draw attention. I'm very outspoken, and in my world that's not unusual. For example, in your world, if a woman speaks her mind, unless she is of high rank, like Queen Elizabeth, she could get into trouble, or worse, be labeled a witch."

"My mother would like your world." The words were said with regret and sadness.

"Don't worry. We will find a way to save your

mother. I promise." She prayed she could keep her word.

Devon shivered again and rubbed her arms. "We should be safe for a while here. Everyone in the castle is busy dressing for the night's activities and would have already selected their gowns."

"You are cold." Graham reached for a green velvet cloak and draped it over her shoulders. "You should change out of your wet clothes."

Images of how the man standing before her would look naked poured into her thoughts. She winked. "You first."

He chuckled, lifting her chin and lowering his head until his lips were a breath away. "Your wish is my command, milady."

His words sent warm shivers over her skin. She knew she should be concentrating on developing a plan, but his eyes were a milk chocolate brown that warmed her to the tips of her toes. She melted into his kiss, his embrace, and the feel of his body against hers. The smells of woodsmoke, leather, cinnamon, flour, and nutmeg merged with the aroma of malted barley, making her dizzy with desire and hope.

She should be afraid. They'd been attacked and Lord Basil's soldiers were still looking for them. But in this moment, wrapped in Graham's arms, she felt safe, safer with Graham than she'd ever felt in her life. Her thoughts were irrational, but they took hold nonetheless and wouldn't let go. She knew Graham would protect her with his life. She had seen the proof firsthand. He was everything she'd ever wanted, and many things she'd never thought she needed.

"Am I interrupting?" Charlotte stood in the center of the room, chuckling softly.

Startled, Devon broke away from Graham's embrace. For a brief moment, in his arms, she'd lost all sense of time and place. The present flowed back, and with regret she regained her footing.

She rushed toward Charlotte and hugged her. "How did you know I'd be here?"

Charlotte's smile widened as she nodded toward Graham. "Thank you for keeping Devon safe. And as for why I'm here... This room was where we planned to meet if there was trouble. Bran told me he overheard soldiers talking about a cookbook, and Mr. Lum confirmed the story. Are you any closer to finding out who stole it?"

Graham gave a slight bow. "It was I who stole the cookbook. Lord Basil sent me here to find the cookbook and steal it in exchange for my mother's freedom. It seemed a simple exchange until I met Devon and realized she was also in danger." He pulled the cookbook from the folds of his tunic and frowned. "It is wet and smells like beer. Normally, I like the smell, but not in this case. Do you think it is ruined?"

Devon retrieved the cookbook from Graham and turned the pages gently. It wasn't ruined, but beer from the exploding barrels had soaked the edges and seeped into some of the pages, blurring parts of the recipes. Her heart sank. Even if she could figure out the right spell, she still didn't know which recipe held the power to send her forward in time. Her heart ached at the thought of returning and leaving Graham behind. She pushed down the somber reality and refocused. With some of the pages ruined, their one bargaining chip was potentially gone.

Right now, they had more important things to consider. "We are the only ones who know the cookbook might be compromised. Charlotte, I'll need you to find another cookbook about the same size as this one and copy the image of the two crossed spoons on the cover. We'll give Lord Basil the fake one. The only question is where and when we will make the exchange."

"How about the Queen's After Party?" Charlotte suggested.

Graham nodded. "I will send word to Lord Basil that I will only deliver the cookbook to him if my mother is present at the After Party. He would never risk making a scene in front of the Queen."

"I have another idea," Charlotte said. "Perhaps a scene is exactly what is called for, and we'll need everyone's help for it to succeed. Devon, you are always referring to me as your Fairy Godmother. I may not be able to change a pumpkin into a coach, but I don't need to. Choose one of the gowns in this room. You will be attending the Queen's After Party with Sir Graham."

Chapter Seventeen

A short time later, Devon rested her hand on Graham's arm as they proceeded into the Great Hall where the Queen's After Party was underway. Mr. Lum had arranged a meeting with Lord Basil, and although the plan was straightforward, the preparations were as detailed as the cookie wedding cake she had made for the Dundee wedding. If Charlotte's plan was to succeed, everything had to be as exact as a recipe for a meringue cookie. One misstep and everything would fall apart. But unlike the cookie wedding cake she'd created, if something went wrong tonight, Devon couldn't frost it over with thick icing. She rubbed her neck, feeling the weight of the evening and its consequences press down on her shoulders.

To calm her frayed nerves, she smoothed her hands over the mistletoe green silk fabric of the dress she'd selected. Charlotte had insisted Devon wear a dress fit for a noblewoman, as Lord Basil was looking for a servant, and this one certainly covered that base. It was the most beautiful gown she'd ever worn. Whipping cream-white pearls were sewn into the bodice and crystal and emeralds into the long, flowing silk skirts. The dress was fit for a princess and must have cost a small fortune. Like many of those in attendance, Devon wore a mask that matched her gown, and the intensity of the color helped create the illusion that her eyes were both green.

The Great Hall had been transformed. Red fabric covered the walls, and crystal chandeliers were suspended from the ceiling on gold chains wrapped in red velvet. Garlands of holly with fat red berries were draped over mantels and framed doorways and archways. Hundreds of nobles and guests of the Queen, dressed in jewel-toned silks, satins, and fur trims, crowded the room like ornaments on a Christmas tree. In all the years Devon had spent helping her family cater events, she'd never seen a place decorated this elaborately. She loved everything about the room.

Tables and chairs, draped in white silk, formed the perimeter and highlighted the focal point of the event— the gingerbread castle. Charlotte had covered it with a gold cloth for maximum dramatic effect and stood beside Mr. Lum. Charlotte and Mr. Lum were also dressed in the fanciest clothes their station would allow, as they had a critical part to play.

The timing had to be flawless if the plan was to work. Devon had read enough historical accounts to understand that double crossing and betrayal were common. First, Lord Basil would suspect a double cross and demand proof he had the right cookbook. Graham had made demands of his own and insisted his mother be present for the exchange. Once Lord Basil had possession of the book, they'd lose their bargaining power.

Graham leaned down to whisper in Devon's ear. "Lord Basil has arrived."

Devon nodded and moved a short distance away from Graham to blend in with a group of noblewomen dressed in multi-colored gowns similar in style to hers.

Lord Basil appeared at the entrance to the Great Hall

dressed in black and looking like a giant Ken doll cake topper. He scanned the room with a predator's gaze seeking his prey, and as hoped, he glossed over Devon as though she were just one of the numerous noblewomen in attendance. But also, as expected, he fixated on Graham as a trumpet blared, announcing the Queen's arrival.

Devon had seen countless portraits of Queen Elizabeth I, and the debate around her appearance was as varied as the historical accounts. First glance left little doubt of the Queen's regal stature. Her golden gown was covered with diamonds as numerous as the stars in the sky. Ropes of pearls hung from her slender neck to her waist, and a crown of rubies and emeralds rested on her head. There was strength and courage in the lift of her chin and the way she walked toward the gingerbread castle.

Devon focused on the Queen's eyes. They were the eyes of someone who had endured great sadness and survived. Shrewd eyes that recognized a friend or an enemy and had known love and sacrifice. History wrote Elizabeth was one of the greatest rulers of her time. Devon believed she would have been a great leader in any century.

Devon had read the Queen had varied interests, including occasionally consulting Star Charts in order to predict favorable times to make decisions. Because the Queen had an open mind on such matters, Devon worried what the Queen's reaction would be to what they had planned. The wrong reaction might prove deadly.

****

Graham took his position a short distance from the entrance to the Great Hall, waiting for Lord Basil to approach. He had been delayed by one of his soldiers, no doubt reporting they hadn't been able to find Devon. Graham's contact with Lord Basil over the last few hours had been written messages only. Graham had insisted they meet and make the exchange in a public place, and the most public place was the Queen's After Party. It was a testament to Lord Basil's obsession with the cookbook that he'd accepted Graham's conditions.

The Queen was near the gingerbread display, talking to Charlotte and Mr. Lum. Graham was too far away to overhear what Mr. Lum was saying to the Queen, but from Charlotte's pleased expression, Mr. Lum was staying on script. The rehearsed speech wasn't far from the truth. Mr. Lum would give Charlotte, Devon, and Graham credit for building the gingerbread castle. Departing from the truth, Mr. Lum would claim that the cookbook belonged to Lord Basil.

Lord Basil, his business concluded, hurried over to Graham. His cold eyes narrowed as he drew near. "I've upheld my part of the bargain. Where is the cookbook?"

Graham forced calm into the tone of his voice. "As I mentioned, I demand proof my mother still lives."

"As you wish." Lord Basil indicated a large balcony overlooking the gardens, and one of his soldiers drew back the drapes covering the glass doors. Standing on the balcony was a woman draped in a hooded, shadow-dark cape. Her hands were shackled in front of her, and she was guarded by Lord Basil's men. She shook her head, and the hood fell back, exposing chin-length white hair that tumbled around her face and shimmered like incandescent pearls in the moonlight. Her eyes were shaped like almonds and her skin youthful, despite her white hair.

Graham recognized his mother at once. Like the Queen, Graham's mother was a woman people underestimated at their peril. Lord Basil had made a strategic error. Although his mother was guarded and shackled, she was outside in the elements where she could tap into her magic.

His mother's gaze turned toward Graham as she gave a slight shake of her head. Her message to him was clear. She did not want him to give Lord Basil the cookbook, no matter if the decision might cost her life.

Graham gave the slightest of nods in return, praying that she understood there was a bigger plan afoot. He turned toward Lord Basil and kept his voice devoid of emotion. "The cookbook is with the gingerbread castle created for the After Party. The Queen has been informed that you are its owner and is eager to thank you."

"I underestimated you, Sir Graham. You selected a public place for the exchange. But once I have the cookbook in my possession, how do I unlock its magic? Your mother claims she does not have the skill. What is more, the woman named Devon, with one blue eye and one green, has conveniently disappeared. And yet you boast that you find lost things."

Graham allowed Lord Basil's words to cling to the air. The man's own words played into Graham's hands. "As you say, I find lost things. We do not need my mother or Devon. I have learned how to unlock the secrets of the cookbook's magic myself."

Graham pretended to ignore Lord Basil's gasp of excitement as he motioned for the man to follow him closer to the entrance of the garden's balcony where his mother was guarded. He wanted to make sure his mother overheard what he was about to say.

He lifted his voice. "The gingerbread castle on display for the Queen's After Party is connected to the cookbook's magic, as it was created from one of the recipes. I will tell you its secrets once my mother's iron shackles are removed and she is released."

Lord Basil hesitated as he looked toward Graham's mother. "You cannot believe I am that gullible. I will agree to unlock your mother's shackles, but she will remain under guard until I have proof I can wield the cookbook's magic."

Graham tamped down his eagerness to proceed. It must look to Lord Basil that he was considering this condition. He waited the length of another heartbeat and nodded. "Agreed."

Lord Basil nodded toward the guards. When the shackles were unlocked, Graham continued.

"According to Devon, the gingerbread castle on display is connected to a magical recipe in the cookbook that I have marked with a ribbon. You must recite the recipe aloud while standing near the gingerbread castle. When you finish reading, the cookbook will recognize you as its master, and then you are free to make any demands of it you desire."

Graham waited for his words to take hold. Would Lord Basil believe him?

Lord Basil's gaze narrowed. "It seems so simple."

Graham recited the words his mother had taught him when he had learned she was a witch. "Magic is like most skills. Talent plays a part, but patience and practice are the true keys to success."

Chapter Eighteen

Devon ducked behind a trio of pine trees that had been cut down from the castle's estate and brought into the Great Hall as part of the Christmas decorations. Ornaments, shaped from sugar-glass into the form of icicles, dripped from the branches and sparkled like prisms in the candlelight. They added to the setting's atmosphere of enchantment and reflected in the red and green plates and goblets also made from sugar-glass. The decorations were breathtaking, and Devon regretted that if the diversion succeeded, the confusion might destroy all this beauty.

From her vantage point, Lord Basil had concluded his conversation with Graham and was making his way through the crowd toward the Queen. Graham had moved closer to the garden balcony where his mother was guarded. The moment the diversion was created, the plan was for Graham to free his mother and take her to safety.

If all went well, she and Graham had agreed to meet in town in the morning. What had gone unsaid was that neither of them believed there would be a next day for them. Circumstance would force Graham to go his way and Devon hers.

She felt empty inside at the thought of never seeing Graham again, but she couldn't think about that right now. She had to focus. She pressed her hand against the cookbook she had hidden against her laced bodice, hoping its presence would give her strength. Generations of her ancestors had used the spells in the cookbook to create only good magic, and she would not allow that to change.

She glanced toward Lord Basil. It was taking him longer than expected to reach the Queen and the area where the gingerbread castle was on display. It wasn't unusual for the Queen to get bored and leave a celebration early, and they needed her here for their plan to work. Noblemen and women kept interrupting Lord Basil, seeking his advice, or praising him for some campaign he'd won.

Devon looked at Graham for assistance. He had moved onto the garden balcony and was in a heated conversation with his mother. Charlotte and Mr. Lum were also engaged in conversation, and she couldn't get their attention.

On his slow path toward the Queen, Lord Basil paused a short distance away from her. She hid from view and pressed against the boughs of the fragrant pine trees. Purple eyes stared back at her.

Startled, Devon drew back. Gossamer-thin wings lay flat against a red gown as the fairy winked. Devon smiled at the adorable creature. This was the fairy she'd animated from a cookie and had seen recently outside. It was as though the fairy was watching over her. The fairy smiled back as though reassuring Devon to be patient. Devon smiled again and whispered for the fairy to be careful.

In what seemed to take forever, Lord Basil finally reached his destination, and when he did, the Queen nodded, and Mr. Lum removed the gold cloth covering the gingerbread castle. It shone like liquid copper. The cookie cutouts of painted nobles, fairies, and knights stood as still as statues, as though holding their breath.

The Queen clapped, laughing with delight, releasing the tension. Although the gingerbread castle was beautifully crafted, the only opinion that mattered was the Queen's.

A collective sigh was followed by the sounds of ohs and ahs lifting in the air. Cheers, and the deafening sound of clapping, erupted as people circled the display to get a better view. The Queen announced two of the three creators were unavailable but was assured that Lord Basil, the owner of the cookbook, was present. She motioned for him to join her, and with his head held high, he strutted forward to take a bow.

Lord Basil bowed to the Queen and shared a brief conversation. She called for silence in the Great Hall, and with her nod, he picked up the fake cookbook. He opened it to the page marked with a ribbon and read aloud.

"To make gingerbread," he began in a loud, confident voice, "mix together flour, cinnamon, nutmeg, ginger…"

Lord Basil's reading aloud the recipe was Devon's signal to begin.

Hidden behind the decorated trees, and with one hand pressed against her bodice where she'd kept the cookbook and the other raised in the direction of the gingerbread castle, she ordered the gingerbread cookies to animate. She held her breath. Nothing happened.

She was about to try again when the gingerbread castle shuddered as though a gentle breeze were weaving through its walls.

The fairies were the first to animate, and they fluttered like multi-colored butterflies around the walls of the gingerbread castle. The fairy from the pine trees where Devon was hiding darted to join her friends. Cookie-shaped noblemen and women animated and began dancing in the gingerbread castle's ballroom. Lord Basil, the Queen, and her guests were stunned into silence.

This was the distraction they had planned.

Slowly, Devon backed away from the pine trees and moved toward the windows to make her escape. She knew the silence wouldn't last. People were in shock. As soon as it registered that cookies had come to life, panic would rush in, and she needed to leave the Great Hall before that happened.

Then one of the cookie knights grew taller.

She froze. That was new.

Devon had expected to animate the knight cookies along with the others, not make them grow. The silver frosting she had used when decorating the knight turned to polished armor and there was a red feather-type plume on his helmet. He looked so real.

Continuing to grow, he jumped down from the display table and lumbered, stiff legged, toward Lord Basil. How had she done that? She reviewed the spell she had cast and couldn't remember saying anything about enlarging the cookies. But then, the spell with the beer barrels hadn't gone smoothly either.

Graham reached for Devon's side. "We have to go. Charlotte and Mr. Lum have already left, and I've taken care of my mother's guards."

She smiled, feeling the warmth she always felt when Graham was close. She nodded, moving with him around the stunned guests, whose gazes were locked on the gingerbread castle. She only half registered what Graham had said. All she could think about was that he'd come back for her.

In the next instant, tables and chairs crashed to the floor, and she heard the sounds of glass breaking and people screaming. Realization that the cookies were enchanted had settled in and fear replaced shock. People screamed and rushed out of the Great Hall. It was mass chaos.

The gingerbread knight was life-size and had turned wonder into panic. Even the fairies were fleeing, rushing to open windows or balconies. Lord Basil cowered against a wall and stared at the gingerbread knight towering over him. Screams were replaced with shouts, accusing Lord Basil of sorcery.

A blast of cold air greeted her as she followed Graham outside onto the garden balcony. The soldiers who had been guarding Graham's mother lay unconscious. Graham bolted the doors and reached for Devon's hand as he led her toward the stairs that wound down to the shadow-draped gardens below.

A woman with white hair stood on the top step with both hands raised in the direction of the Great Hall. Stacks of bead bracelets dangled from her wrists, chiming together like musical notes as she struggled to keep her arms raised. "I can't hold the magic much longer."

The woman looked familiar to Devon, but she couldn't place her.

Graham put his hand on the woman's shoulder gently. "Mother, you can stop now. We have to leave."

The woman lowered her arms and smiled. "Devon.

We meet again. You have a powerful gift. I only added a tweak here and there to enhance the magic."

Devon recognized the warm smile. "Now I remember. You're the shopkeeper. You gave me the cookbook."

A trumpet blared over the mass confusion in the Great Hall, silencing those who remained. In the next instant, the Queen's voice rang out clear and steady, filled with anger. "We accuse Lord Basil of sorcery. Take him to the tower!"

Devon looked toward the windows. There was no sign of the giant gingerbread knight as guards marched Lord Basil away.

"We need to leave." Graham motioned for them to take the stairs into the gardens and then to a clearing, where three horses were tethered. With a nod of his head, his mother moved toward the horses, as Graham held back.

As her heart raced from adrenaline, Devon took in great gulps of air to catch her breath. She had so many questions, beginning with how Graham's mother was involved. The question paled in comparison to how she was feeling about Graham. "You came back for me," she blurted.

He took her hands in his. "How could I not? I love you. You are my world."

"Charlotte? Mr. Lum?"

"All safe and headed to my mother's holdings in Scotland. Bran and his family as well. It's best they are not around when things settle down."

He was calm, reassuring, and thinking of everyone's safety. A safe harbor in the midst of a wild storm.

"There was a giant gingerbread knight."

"My mother's doing. I disagreed, but she felt it necessary to create an extra layer of panic. This is where we part ways. Lord Basil will be accused of sorcery and imprisoned." He paused. "My mother assures me she can help you decipher the magic of the cookbook so you can return to your own time."

This was the moment she had dreaded. She took in more gulps of air as her heart raced out of control. This was the moment she would be forced to decide. Return to her own time and the familiar and safe? Or stay behind, knowing that if Lord Basil escaped, she would likely be his prime target?

The moon shone full and bright in the crisp night air, illuminating Graham as though holding him in the palm of its hand. Silence wrapped around her. The Great Hall had cleared, and Graham waited as though she had all the time in the world to decide. She might be able to delay her decision until the morning. She could ask him to spend the night making love. They'd make promises to each other that they knew they couldn't keep.

Her eyes blurred with tears. She didn't want one night with him. She wanted a lifetime.

"Please, come with me."

He shook his head. "I wish with all my heart I could go with you, but I cannot travel with you to your time. There is much about my past you do not know. What I can tell you is that I love you and you have changed me forever. The true magic in this world is love. Your loving me has made me whole."

She moved into his arms and felt their warmth envelope her like a fire on a cold winter night or the aroma of baked bread fresh from the oven. He believed that the secrets of his past stood between them and made him unworthy of love. Yet, to Devon, it was his believing he was not worthy of love that made her love him more.

"I love you with all my heart and can't bear to think of my life without you. Your loving me has made me whole as well." She stood on tiptoes and put her arms around his neck. "I'm not leaving. I want to stay with you."

"What about your home?"

"My home is with you."

Snowdrop Cookie Wishes

by

Laura Strickland

Christmas Cookies

Dedication

To all those who believe, as do I,
that hope and love are one and the same

Chapter One

Gjerhold, Denmark, Christmas 1531

The big stone kitchen smelled of spices, hints of faraway places Lissi had never seen. The warmth of Egypt issued from a small measure of cinnamon. The hot sun of Portugal lay locked in a few grains of mace, and the exotic potency of far distant eastern isles wafted from a pinch of cloves. Remnants of lands Lissi couldn't dream of visiting, especially now, lay spread across the table here in this cold, northern place.

So little remained. Lissi remembered other Christmases when her father, alderman of the town, had ordered a wealth of such supplies well in advance of the season. Lissi, along with her mother and her younger sister, Dagny, spent days baking, filling this room and, ja, all the house with fragrance. No effort seemed too fantastical then. Towering cakes, sweetmeats, and wafered pastries came from this kitchen, to gladden tables throughout the town.

A kind of tradition it was, one that brought much joy to many.

One that, like so much else, had now died.

Ever since Lissi could remember, her parents—Viggo and Sussi Johansen—had taught her that Christmas was about giving rather than receiving. Oh, they exchanged gifts, small ones. But true pleasure lay in making certain their neighbors in this tiny village shared in their plenty.

"I am a fortunate man," Papa often said, with his big, wide smile. "I have so much to fill my table, and my heart." Then he would put one arm around Lissi and another around Dagny, hugging them tight. He would plant a kiss on Mama's cheek, and make her laugh.

A tear came to Lissi's eye, blurring the skimpy collection of spices set out upon the table. The plague had arrived last year—stemming, some said, from a ghost ship that had gone aground at Jutland. At first, Papa had insisted they would be safe here in Gjerhold. He had closed the village to visitors, but it was too late. The black death had already sneaked in.

Last Christmas, no one had celebrated. Lissi barely remembered that holiday season. Now the sickness, having scourged them and taken what it wanted, had moved on. Many slept in the churchyard, including members of nearly every household. No one went to church any more, and the fine stone building stood closed. Those left in Gjerhold—the survivors—had little heart for festivities.

But life, as Mama always used to say, moved on. And good folk needed to move with it, sometimes against steep odds.

Mama, the daughter of a humble farmer, never expected to marry the wealthiest man in town. But Papa, as he loved to tell Lissi and Dagny, had taken one look at her golden hair and smiling blue eyes and lost his heart.

Light had come into his life on that day, he insisted. He'd spent countless days thereafter spreading that light around. Making sure people had enough, and maybe just a bit extra, to make them happy.

A tradition Lissi, despite her poor store of spices, ached to carry on this year. If she could shine even a dim ray of light into this darkness—

"What are you doing?"

The strident question came from the kitchen doorway. Lissi turned and saw old Mitte standing there with her turban wrapped around her head and a forbidding frown on her face.

Mitte had been Lissi's nurse, and Dagny's. Mama's also, years ago. A kindly woman, if stern, she'd lived as part of the family and shared in the abundance of love in this house. She'd changed, though, since she and Lissi had tended every other member of the family and buried them.

Lissi could not say why just the two of them had survived. Mitte had already been aged when the sickness struck, yet she'd never fallen ill.

Instead, it had chosen Papa, so hale and hearty. Lissi herself had taken ill but recovered, while Mama and Dagny did not.

She could find no sense in it.

Lissi acknowledged now, regarding her old nurse, that not all of Mitte had survived. Her glow of happiness had surely been lost.

Precisely what Lissi ached to replace, this year.

When she did not speak, Mitte marched to the table where she eyed Lissi's collection. "Girl, have you gone mad, hauling out these things? You know how precious they are. We have so little left, and you can be sure we will get no more."

"I know that." Mitte's harsh tone, so Lissi assured herself, stemmed from nothing so much as her grief.

"But I have an idea."

Mitte shot her one discerning look from beneath gray brows before she said, "Well, best to put it away, girl, with the rest of this. It is no time for foolishness."

"No?" Lissi turned to face the woman. "What is it time for, then?"

"Prayer. Endurance."

"Mitte, it is Christmas."

"Christmas is for the living—"

"Which you and I are, still. I know…" Lissi reached out and clasped Mitte's arm. "You buried your heart with Mama."

"And Dagny. And your papa. All were dear to me."

"And me." Lissi said it softly. "But we remain. And we need to find a way to carry on. I thought—I thought I would bake some cookies."

Mitte stared. "You have indeed gone mad."

"Not at all."

"Those ovens haven't fired in a year, except to bake our bread."

"I know."

"We haven't the ingredients for cookies. Not enough butter. Almost no flour."

"Ja."

"So." Mitte waved a hand wildly. "You would waste what little we do have on frivolities? How are we to eat, come the new year, eh?"

That was a problem. No new supplies had come into the village for some time. The local farmers, having lost so many members of their families, had not grown enough grain this past season to keep Ole Andersen, the miller, busy.

Father's coffers had dwindled so alarmingly,

Lissi—who'd been raiding them without compunction—doubted she could even order from farther afield.

"But Mitte, I have been wondering how we are to survive in the new year without hope in our hearts. You remember the happiness Papa used to spread when he distributed the things we made throughout the village."

Mitte's harsh expression softened. "I do. A time of great joy, it was. And, girl, your heart is in the right place. But those of us left here are lost in grief."

"All the more reason to do something—something to lift that sorrow."

"You think a few cookies can replace all that's been lost? A husband, a parent? A child?"

"No. But I thought if I baked some magic into these cookies—"

"Magic!" Mitte scoffed. "All that nonsense your mama used to spout, I suppose."

"It was not nonsense. Mama believed. Everything we made, so she insisted, had a measure of magic in it. Good wishes. Love."

"Your mama was made for love, she was." Two tears rolled down Mitte's wrinkled cheeks. "That such a soul should lie beneath the sod—"

"Her soul does not lie there. It is gathering light, in heaven, as her heart did here on earth. Mitte, do you not see? I want to spend some of that light in Gjerhold this season. Our neighbors need it. Because we cannot exist forever in the darkness. We have to be able to step forward, somehow."

Mitte caressed Lissi's hair. "You are a good girl. So long as you are here, your blessed mama is not gone too far from me."

"Then you'll help make the cookies?"

Mitte's gaze measured the supplies on the table. "To make enough for the whole village? We are not many, but you will need far more than that."

Before Lissi could protest, Mitte hurried on, saying, "We have not even firewood enough to stoke those ovens properly. They are stone cold."

"One oven," Lissi admitted ruefully. "I doubt we can manage much more."

"I doubt you can manage that. What about the flour, eh? The sugar?"

"I have been thinking about that. We have still a measure of honey."

"Precious little."

"I thought if I went to our neighbors and begged what they may have—"

"You, to go begging? The daughter of Viggo Johansen?"

"I am no better than anyone else. And it is for a good cause."

"You will have trouble convincing anyone else of that."

Lissi hoped not.

"As for flour—"

"Ja, that could prove difficult. I suppose I will have to go see the miller, to do my begging for flour."

"Ole Andersen, who has lost his wife and one of his daughters?"

Lissi shrugged. "We have all lost so much. I will convince him that is why we should share."

Mitte snorted. "Folk cannot share what they do not have."

"We have all, still, a measure of love."

"That, my girl, is where you are wrong, as I'm sure

you soon shall see."

Nay, Lissi thought. She just needed to believe, believe hard enough.

Chapter Two

The mill wheel needed repair—again. Ole Andersen lay on his back in the chilly bed, his arm bent across his eyes, and tried to find the strength to rise.

Another morning of another day. His daughter, Hanne, only seven years old, lay in her cot in the next room—still asleep, or so he hoped. She'd finally stopped crying every night for her mama and younger sister. But the child rarely smiled.

Perhaps because he, Ole, rarely did.

He uncovered his eyes and stared at the rough ceiling. How many days left before the holiday? He'd lost count, and it left him feeling helpless. He supposed he should make an effort for Hanne's sake, try to make her a little gift as he used to do other years. But few resources remained.

He needed to rise from the bed, repair the mill wheel in case someone came with grain for their Christmas bread.

But his emotions weighed upon him. Grief, ja. But even worse did he find the loneliness. A young man still, he did not thrive on a dearth of company.

He sat up abruptly when a knock sounded at the outer door. His hair, which hadn't been cut since Dorrit died, flopped over his forehead, and he clawed it out of the way hastily. Who could that be? And how late had he lain abed? Far too late, for now muddy sunlight crept over the windowsill.

The knock came again.

"Papa?" Hanne called from the next room.

"I am coming!"

Clad in his britches and undershirt, in which he'd slept, he hurried to the door and hauled it open.

A woman stood there, a small woman, only about as high as his ear. When the door flew open she looked up at him—grave blue eyes in a fine oval of a face.

Mistress Lissi it was, from the alderman's house.

"Goodness," he grunted. What could have brought her here on such a chilly morning? Cold it was, and the stinging air swept in at him. Snow had fallen during the night and covered the ground.

"Forgive me," she said. "I went first to the mill." She indicated the structure next door. "But nobody was there."

"Ah, ja. Will you step in?" Whatever might have happened to change their world, the alderman's daughter still warranted courtesy.

Viggo Johansen's daughter stepped in. The house felt chilly, and shame touched Ole.

"Papa?" Hanne questioned again. She'd tiptoed out from her room, her feet bare.

"Go get dressed, angel, ja? It is but a customer, I think."

As the child ran off, Ole turned back to his visitor and eyed her. "Ja?"

"I come, Master Andersen, not to bring you business, but to beg your generosity."

"Eh?" Hastily, Ole tucked his nightshirt into his trousers. "Pardon?"

She glanced around the room, and Ole's shame

deepened. How long since he'd emptied the ashes from the fire, or swept the floor? How long since he'd even given those things a thought?

Mistress Lissi's gaze returned to him. "It is nearly Christmas. You will remember the gifts my father used to distribute at this time of year."

"Ja, of course." Dorrit and the girls had looked forward to it. All the village had.

Mistress Lissi pushed the hood of her cloak back onto her shoulders, revealing dull golden hair, well-braided. "I would like to do something like that this year."

"Ach. But—"

"I know, it cannot possibly be so grand. There aren't very many of us left. But I thought if I baked one batch of cookies, just one…"

"Ah, mistress, it is a worthy idea, yet…" He spread his hands. "No one has the heart."

She lifted her eyebrows. "That is the root of the problem, as I see it. To thrive, the heart needs joy. And I wish to provide some."

"Joy." He repeated the word as if he'd never before heard it. "And you think a—a cookie can do this?"

"It cannot hurt. I have assembled some supplies at home. I have a measure of spices, honey—I do not have flour, at least not enough to spare from our bread." She looked at him meaningfully.

"And you come to me?"

"You are the miller. I thought—hoped—"

"Ah." Ole's thoughts raced. He had a small store of flour, very little. It consisted of supplies belonging to those who never picked up their orders after the sickness struck the village. Old and stale, it might not do for what she wanted.

"I will need some sugar, also," she went on as if in defiance of his doubt. "I thought to make Snowdrop Cookies. As I say, I have the proper spices, and they were always the most popular of what we baked." She gave him a tentative smile. "Besides, they are such a symbol of—hope. Are they not?"

Hope. She kept repeating that word. And for what should he, Ole, hope? An end to his loneliness? A life lived, after losing nearly everything?

Hanne, having dressed and donned her shoes, ran back into the room and pressed close to Ole's side.

Gazing into Mistress Lissi's wide, blue eyes, he said, "I have not much flour."

"I do not need much. I will not be able to bake enough for everyone. But I thought if I baked good wishes inside, and gave them to those among us who have been hit the hardest—I could make sure you get one. For—" She nodded at Hanne.

Ole's throat closed. For weeks it had haunted him, the knowledge that he would be able to give his daughter almost nothing, this Christmas. Dorrit used to bake, ja, and he, Ole, would make each of their girls a toy. The house would be filled with greenery and handmade decorations.

He cupped Hanne's head tenderly in his hand and drew her closer. For a terrible instant, he thought he might shed tears, here before the alderman's daughter.

His voice softened when he said, "You are a kind woman, Mistress Johansen."

Her expression brightened. "You think it a good idea, then?"

"I think it a very good idea, indeed."

"Mitte—she's my nurse—says it's a waste of the few ingredients I have left."

Ole stared past her at the snow dusting the ground, just like sugar on the legendary Snowdrop Cookies. He said, "I think—I think there are times when to splurge is everything."

"Ja." Her face lit in a sweet smile. "And Christmas is one of those times."

"I agree."

"Thank you, Master Andersen. It is fine to know someone agrees with me."

"I will search the mill and see what I can find. If I come up with a measure, I will bring it to you."

"Do not take too long, eh? Christmas is in two days."

"I will do it this very afternoon."

Impulsively, she reached out and touched his hand. "*Tak. Tak*!"

Before Ole could react, she turned and ran off, her cloak flaring out behind her in the clear morning air.

He watched her down the trail and out of sight before he picked Hanne up in his arms.

"Papa?" Hanne craned to look back after Lissi. "Was that lady magical?"

At the verge of denying it, Ole caught himself. "Well, I don't know, poppet. I guess we will have to wait and see."

What child didn't deserve to believe in magic at Christmastime?

Chapter Three

Lissi returned home with Ole Andersen's promise in her ear and a tiny glow of warmth in her heart. She still had much to sort out, including sufficient firewood for her oven so she might accomplish this task that had now gained such importance to her.

She would also need to find more honey and—most precious of all—the white sugar for sprinkling on top. She supposed in a pinch she could make the cookies without that finishing touch, but they would not look like snowdrops, would they?

Snowdrops were heralds of spring, and the life that returned with it. The first flowers to appear, they often pushed their heads up through a blanket of snow. Mama had told Lissi, as they baked together, that the flowers provided proof that light would return to the world after a hard winter.

If ever a village needed a return to light, it was Gjerhold.

The miller might supply her flour, but where could she obtain that sugar? She still fretted over the question later that afternoon, when a knock came at the kitchen door.

She opened it to find Ole Andersen standing there, his hat already removed from his overly long, light brown hair, his gaze serious.

Nothing about the sight of him should make Lissi's

heart bound the way it did, except gladness that he'd kept his word. For he held a small sack in one hand.

"Come in, come in. did you not bring your daughter?"

"She is with Mistress Krupp, our neighbor." He stamped the snow from his boots before he stepped into the kitchen.

A tall man, was Ole Andersen, knit together from long, sturdy bones, though at the moment he looked far too gaunt. Lissi remembered him, of course, from the time before the sickness as a happy young man with a blooming family and a ready smile. Everyone in the village liked Ole Andersen.

Now, new lines bit deep into his broad face. But his eyes—ja, those held kindness as he peered at Lissi from between brown lashes. Gray eyes they were, that had seen much sorrow but still dared to offer compassion.

"I have brought you some flour." He set the sack on the clean table. Lissi had put all her carefully husbanded spices away. "It is the best of what I had in store, though not as much as I would like."

Lissi clapped her hands. "Oh, thank you."

"And..." He opened his coat and from inside produced a much smaller sack. "I have this."

She shot him a look of inquiry.

"I remembered that Mistress Hensen was planning her wedding when..." For an instant the light in his eyes faded. "When the trouble came. She had got flour from me—ground extra fine—for a cake. This is sugar she did not use."

"Ach! And she is willing to give it up for us?"

Gravely, Ole said, "She assured me she has no use for it now and sends it with her blessing."

210

"This is wonderful! Master Andersen, it is as if our plan is meant to succeed."

He leaned against the edge of the table. "It is good to bring some light into our lives now, at the darkest time."

He did not mean the winter. She nodded. "As I say, I will not be able to make as many cookies as Mama and Papa did, not enough for everyone in the village. But I am hoping one, perhaps, for each household. I hope that may spread some joy. I suppose it is foolish, after all."

"No, Mistress Johansen, it is not." He smiled, and his grave face momentarily shone. "You bake your magic in there. It is what we need."

"Thank you. Thank you for helping me. I will make sure your Hanne gets a cookie."

He nodded and quickly turned for the door. Were those tears Lissi caught in his eyes?

****

Some of Lissi's best memories involved Mama, Dagny, and herself baking in this kitchen, to the accompaniment of stories and laughter. Often Mama sang as she stirred the ingredients or kneaded the bread. She would tell them tales of folk who lived long ago, of trolls and giants, and brave, honest men. She spoke of the magic woven into the fabric of the world, and she made Lissi believe.

"I wish you were here with me now, Mama," Lissi whispered the next morning, as she mixed up her cookie batter. "I dare not make a mistake."

Nay, for each cookie had to be perfect, a gift—a small package of good wishes. Limited as her supplies were, she could not start over.

That meant she had to stoke the oven, built in beside

211

the fire, to the perfect temperature. She could afford to burn not so much as a crumb. Undercook nothing. For tomorrow was Christmas Eve, and by rights, she should take her gifts throughout the village on Christmas morning.

Mitte came into the kitchen and gave her a sharp look. "Well, girl? Do you have everything you need?"

"Ja. It will be a small batch."

"So, how will you decide who is to receive these cookies?"

"I promised one for Ole Andersen's daughter. And I suppose one should go to Thora Hensen, since she donated the sugar. Beyond that, I will have to see how many we have."

"Ach, and who are you to decide whose heart aches the worst? Are you God?"

Suddenly, the old nurse's face broke up into a thousand wrinkles of agony. Lissi watched in horror as the tears came.

Mitte had wept before—they both had as they'd tended Papa and Mama and poor Dagny, so ill that Lissi had prayed for her release at the end. They'd shed tears together above their graves. But this felt different. In the past, despite the tears, Mitte's strength had never broken.

Not, perhaps, till now.

"Ach, Mitte." Lissi put her spoon aside and took the old woman in her arms. "I know we all hurt—none more, and none less. I do not mean to pick and choose so much as follow my heart."

She mopped Mitte's cheeks tenderly. "Perhaps you will get a snowdrop, eh? Each comes with a wish. For what would you wish, Mitte?"

Blue eyes awash with tears, and looking like those

of a young woman, Mitte studied Lissi's face. "Nothing for myself, child. Not for me."

"Well, then, you think about it. I mean to make it clear to those of us here in Gjerhold that wishes are for everyone. We need to begin with making them, for without wishing, the heart dies. And have we not had enough of death?"

"Ja." To Lissi's further surprise, Mitte, never a demonstrative woman, planted a kiss on her forehead. "Now let me help you get that oven stoked. You will never get it right."

Lissi smiled. There was her Mitte, back again. And to be sure, Lissi welcomed whatever assistance she could get.

Chapter Four

"Barely a score of cookies. Perhaps I made them too large." Lissi eyed the sweetmeats laid out across the table. In truth, they numbered only nineteen. An odd count, she acknowledged. And none of them was perfect. As the product of all her hope and care, they appeared rather pitiful.

"They're certainly little enough like your mama's," Mitte allowed. "But considering what you had to work with, I think they look good."

"Do you, truly?"

"Ja, child. When do you mean to take them about?"

"I thought tomorrow, Christmas morning. Folks will be waking to, well, to so little. Ach, Mitte, perhaps this is a bad idea. How can these miserable sweetmeats make up for all that's been lost?"

"You stop that, now."

"Stop what?"

"Doubting yourself. You're doing a lovely thing, trying to spread some good wishes here in Gjerhold. You need to believe. What did your mama always say about that?"

"Believing is what matters. That makes the magic."

For an instant, it felt as if Mama were there in the kitchen with them, bending gracefully over the fire, a smile on her face. The scent of spices brought her close, and the sprinkles of sugar on the table.

"I have heard that word has spread around the village. Already, folk hope they will receive a snowdrop."

"Who?" Lissi stared into Mitte's eyes. "I do not want to disappoint anyone."

"Well, as for that, I have done some calculating. Do you know, there are not so many households left in Gjerhold, where people still survive? Guess how many."

"Nineteen?"

"Just so."

"How can there be so few?"

"You need not ask that, girl. Better to ask instead how you came up with nineteen cookies, exactly. There must be magic in it."

"Mitte!" The old nurse had scoffed at Mama's claims of magic.

Mitte shrugged. "Who knows?"

"Not all these cookies are perfect. And I was hoping to give you one."

"Lissi, I need no sweetmeats. I already have you. You've only to decide who, in each house, gets the gift."

"And the wish. Some households will be easy. There is only one person who has survived."

"I hope their wishes, all their wishes, come true. And what of you, my girl? Will you save a wish for yourself?"

"My only wish, Mitte, is to make other folks happy, the way Papa did."

"Well, child, I think you are well on your way."

****

Ole gazed out at the December afternoon and tried to think of an excuse to stop by the alderman's house.

A lovely day, and no mistake. New-fallen snow

dusted the ground and flocked the trees that surrounded the mill house. After a struggle that morning, he'd succeeded in mending the mill wheel and could hear it now, creaking against the current of the fast-flowing stream.

For the first time since he could remember, he noted the beauty of his world—the sun pouring through the clouds, shedding radiance. The isolated snowflakes that swirled down like sprinkled sugar. Or magic.

Did she truly believe in magic, the alderman's daughter? Could she spread it among those left here in Gjerhold?

He could not say, yet for the first time in a year, he'd been eager to get out of bed that morning. He'd got Hanne up with a smile, and she'd smiled back and asked, "Papa, how long till Christmas?"

"Tomorrow. Christmas is tomorrow, darling."

Ja, and his Hanne was a darling. She had her mother's eyes and a smile—if missing two front teeth at the moment—that would melt stone.

He needed to make sure she smiled more often.

He'd fed Hanne breakfast and shaved with far more care than he'd employed in months. Dorrit had loved his beard, but he was no longer the man he'd been when he had slept in Dorrit's arms, and he'd shaved it off in a fit of grief. His hair, as he saw when he peered into the basin of water he used for a mirror, had become a mop, falling over his collar and brow. Should he attempt to chop it off?

Nay, Dorrit had always done that for him, amid smiles and teasing. The memory remained far too bright.

After breakfast he held out his hand to Hanne. "Come, let us go for a walk."

She looked askance. "Now?"

"Why not? It is a pretty day, and no work for me. It is Christmas Eve."

Hanne brightened perceptibly as they headed out through the village. She lit just like the sun, and swung his hand in hers.

Ole's heart convulsed with love for her. Why had he failed to give her more care, this last year? How not spent all his time and energy on her? The heart of a child grew apace with the days, and revived, so it seemed, with each spilling of love.

Hanne was all he had left. Why had it taken the alderman's daughter to remind him he must cherish her?

They passed the church, still shut up tight, and several houses where folk peered out at them. That, of itself, seemed a miracle. Since the sickness, folk rarely ventured out. Ach, he frequently saw his neighbor, widow Krupp, who helped look after Hanne while he worked. No one else.

Now, Mistress Krupp opened her door and eyed them. Tall and gaunt, she had lost half her weight since her husband died. She hesitated before tiptoeing out through the snow to her gate.

"Master miller, good day."

Ole tipped his hat to her.

"Tell me, Ole Andersen, is it true what we hear? Viggo Johansen's daughter is to hand out cookies, as of old?"

"Not as of old, perhaps, but she's done her best."

"How do you know?"

"I helped supply the flour. And not just cookies. As I understand it, there are wishes baked inside."

"Mercy!"

"Tell me, Mistress Krupp, if you received one, for what would you wish?"

Mistress Krupp glanced behind her, at the dark house. "I am not sure. A wish—a single wish—seems a precious thing. I would have to give that some thought."

"You are a wise woman."

"I have learned some things. But there's no saying I shall receive a wish. That young woman has no liking for me."

"Why do you say that?"

"I remember hollering at her and her sister when they were younger, for plucking flowers out of my garden."

"Well..." Ole winked at the old woman. "I should prepare a wish all the same, just in case you do receive one, in the spirit of Christmas and all."

"Merry Christmas!" Hanne called as they moved away from the gate. And Mistress Krupp gave a smile, the first Ole had seen on her face for over a year.

Indeed, calls of Merry Christmas followed them to the alderman's house. As he had before, Ole went to the back door and knocked.

Lissi Johansen answered it. Her face looked rosy, and when she recognized him, a smile started in her bright blue eyes. It spread until it warmed both of them.

"Ah, Master Ole, come in, come in."

"We were just out for a walk. I do not mean to disturb you, and merely wondered—"

Ole stopped speaking when he saw the cookies laid out across the table. "Ah! They did turn out."

Lissi gave him an anxious look. "You think they look all right?"

"Ja, ja. Wonderful!"

She eased, from relief. "I did not have enough spices or sugar to make more, even with what you brought me from Mistress Hensen. I hope it is enough."

"And each has magic baked inside?"

"Magic, and a wish," Lissi said more confidently, "placed most carefully within."

"That is the important part."

"You think so?"

"I know it." What, Ole wondered, was this strange feeling exploding like a bubble inside his chest, rising to his head? Enthusiasm? Happiness. "How will you distribute them?"

"The same way Mama and Papa did, tomorrow morning. I will place them in a basket and go door to door."

"A fine plan."

"It does not seem much, now that I look at them."

"It is much." Ole smiled. "Everyone is excited. You should hear, they speak of nothing else."

"Well, then." She wiped her hands on her apron before tugging at his elbow, taking him a step from Hanne. Putting her cheek close to his, so close he could feel the warmth of her, she whispered, "I will come first to your house, bright and early, to make sure your little daughter gets hers. After that..." Her gaze met his for a moment. "After that, would you like to accompany me on my rounds?"

"Me?"

"And Hanne, ja. You had a part in this, after all."

Gravely, he told her, "I would like that very much."

"I am sorry—sorry there's no extra cookie for you."

"No matter." Ole already had his wish.

219

Chapter Five

Never had any cookies been handled with such care. Lissi rose before dawn the next morning, lit the kitchen fire, and watched the sun come up. Clear and still, the light flowed over the land like a blessing. It would be a beautiful Christmas Day.

She lined a basket with a linen cloth and placed the cookies tenderly inside. By then, Mitte was up and entered the kitchen with a bundle of red fabric in her hands.

"What is that? Ach!" Tears flooded Lissi's eyes as she recognized the garment in Mitte's arms. "It is Mama's fancy shawl."

"Ja. She always wore this when she and your Papa did their Christmas tour around the village." Mitte stroked the fabric with a loving hand. "It should be yours, now."

Lissi stood silent, head bowed, as the old woman placed the shawl over her hair and wrapped it around her shoulders. "There. Most festive. Are you wearing your good shoes?"

"My good shoes are no longer so good."

"No matter. I gave them a polish last night." Mitte leaned forward and kissed Lissi on the cheek. "Go with God."

Impulsively, Lissi said, "Come with me."

"Nay, I am off to call on that old grump of a

minister, Reverend Pedersen, to see if I can persuade him to open the church this morning. It is time."

"Is it truly, Mitte?"

"Ja. Now go. Enjoy yourself."

Outside, the world sparkled. Each bough of every tree wore a coat of new snow, and birds darted between them like tiny angels. The new sun garnered strength in the sky. Not a breath of wind disturbed the peace.

Directing her feet down the road, Lissi headed for the miller's house. Would Ole and his daughter be awake so early?

Ja, the heavy front door creaked open when she turned up their path. Ole peered out and a big smile came to his face.

Ach, and he looked like a different man, ten years younger, with his coat buttoned up tight and his light brown hair shining.

Lissi smiled back at him. "Merry Christmas, Master Andersen."

"Merry Christmas!"

"I am not too early?"

"Nay. Come in, come in."

The room inside still looked bare and grim, but Lissi could see Ole had made an effort, putting a bright cloth on the table and lighting a candle. Hanne stood there, already dressed and her hair plaited.

"Merry Christmas, Hanne!"

The child's eyes went to the basket over Lissi's arm. No toys in the room this Christmas, and an absence of those she loved, yet light filled her eyes.

It constricted Lissi's throat, thinking on the miracle of that light.

Entering the room, she went down on her knees

221

beside the child.

"It is a beautiful morning, Hanne, as should be. And I have something for you. Tell me, do you believe in magic?"

Hanne looked at Lissi with her blue eyes, perfectly round. "Ja, Mistress Johansen."

Lissi reached into her basket and took out a cookie. "Hold out your hand."

Hanne extended both of them, cupped together.

"Here is a snowdrop cookie, just for you. Snowdrops are the first flowers of spring. They show us hope. There is magic, and a wish, tucked inside this. When you eat the cookie, Hanne, you must spend your wish. But it will only come true if you believe."

Hanne stared at the cookie as if it were a precious gem. Lissi kissed her on the cheek. "Do you know what you will wish for?"

Hanne shot a look at her father and gave a nod.

"Do you want to eat it now?"

"Ja, please and thank you. Must I tell my wish out loud?"

"You do not have to, but you may if you like."

Hanne smiled. "I wish for my papa to be happy again."

Lissi's throat closed completely, rendering it impossible for her to speak. She got to her feet and watched as Hanne consumed her cookie in tiny, careful bites.

Ole cleared his throat. When Lissi glanced at him, he had tears in his eyes.

"The fun is not over, Hanne," Lissi told the child. "Would you like to come through the village with me and gift the other wishes in my basket?"

"Papa too?"

"Papa too, of course."

Ole lifted Hanne onto his shoulder, and the three of them went out into the bright sunlight.

****

Why had Ole never noticed before how beautiful was the alderman's daughter? Ja, she had pretty blue eyes, though many women did. And that golden hair. Neither of those things made her lovely. Rather, her beauty came from her kindness, the smiles she dispensed as they went door to door. The warmth and caring with which she gifted her sweetmeats, making of them precious things.

At the Karlsens' house, where three members of the family survived, they met her with smiles of delight and promptly fell to arguing as to which of them should have the snowdrop.

Each wanted the others to receive the gift. Amid more laughter than Ole had heard in a year, they decided to give it to the youngest, who promptly divided the cookie and made a wish on behalf of the other two.

When Ole, Lissi, and Hanne left their house, they followed along, eager to see what would happen at their neighbors'.

They went next to the house of Mistress Krupp, who so often helped Ole look after Hanne, and who greeted the girl with a big hug. Mistress Krupp, having lost her husband to the sickness, now lived alone and wasted no time in trying to give her wish away to "that sweet child." Hanne informed her patiently she'd already had her wish, and that Mistress Krupp must make one—and believe in order for the magic to work.

Mistress Krupp looked from Ole to Lissi and said

she'd save her wish for later.

"Come with us, mistress," Holger Karlsen invited, and Mistress Krupp took up her shawl.

So it went, from house to house, as they wended their way through the village. Many the house they passed stood dark and abandoned. But at those they approached, doors opened in anticipation and a ready welcome was given.

At each, everyone held his or her breath as Lissi made her explanation and presented her gift. Folks laughed. They wept. Some, too overcome to make a wish at that moment, put their cookie aside for later. Of those who stated their wishes outright, not a single one wished for him or herself. All, all wished for others.

Most joined the now joyful train that made its way to the next house.

The happiness and belief built as they went, until the rowdy group began to chant at each door, "Believe. Believe!"

When had Ole heard so much laughter? He could not remember. Nor had he seen so much of his good neighbors for a very long time. The habit formed during the sickness, of shutting themselves away, had held to keep folks at home.

Until the alderman's daughter hatched her plan. Ole rested his eyes upon her as she stood conversing with old Master Schou, joy on her lips and kindness in her eyes.

Forgive me, Dorrit, he begged silently. Forgive me for finding her beautiful. Was it wrong? Was it too soon for him to see another woman this way?

How could he hope to risk his heart, shattered to pieces? How allow it to care?

The last snowdrop cookie presented, they trailed

back down the road to the church, where they found Mitte standing at the door, waiting for them.

"Come. Come in," she cried.

Mistress Andersen, her empty basket still over her arm, led the way, and the others all followed, singing.

Chapter Six

"A very successful venture, so I do say," Mitte gloated the next morning over breakfast. "Not one person refused his or her gift."

"Or questioned the magic," agreed Lissi, who sat at the table, resting her chin on her hand.

"Why should they question it? It caused Reverend Pedersen to open the doors of the church, did it not?"

"I suspect you were responsible for that."

"No matter. I am thinking they will need to remain open now."

Lissi smiled faintly. It pleased her no end to see Mitte so talkative and high in spirits. She wondered, though, at her own melancholy. Following yesterday's euphoria, she'd awakened this morning with a terrible ache in her heart.

She could not imagine why. Her Christmas cookies had brought as much joy as Mama and Papa's had in days past.

And yet...

Mitte, still rambling on, caught her ear. "Ja, and perhaps soon we shall have a wedding in the church, eh?"

"What?"

"You and young master miller, so I am saying."

Lissi flushed scarlet. "Why would you suggest such a thing?"

Mitte shot her an arch look. "I saw the way he smiled at you, Lissi. With…with light in his eyes."

Lissi, not knowing what to say, held her tongue.

"He is a handsome man. Do you not agree?"

"He is," Lissi answered as calmly as she could manage. "But he has no interest in me. He merely helped to make the Christmas wishes happen."

"Ja, well, much might grow from such helping."

"Nay, Mitte. He is a grief-stricken widower, still in love with his wife."

"And he will love her forever, with part of his heart. The true heart does not forget. But he is a man, and lonely."

"It has not been long, Mitte. Not long enough." Lissi struggled to put her feelings into words. "If you saw anything in his smile, it was his gladness at the day. It was the first time I have heard folk laugh so much since, well, I can barely remember."

Mitte's gaze softened. "It was wonderful, and a time folks will not soon forget. Very well, girl, I will leave the matter in your hands. But—"

"What, Mitte?"

"You did not get a wish."

"I did. I saw folks happy, at least for a time."

"And nothing for yourself?"

"What should I need?"

But her heart whispered otherwise as she rose from the table, went to the kitchen door, and stepped outside. No beautiful day, this. The sky lowered overhead, and the cold air smelled of snow.

Her eyes followed the path that led around the front of the house and eventually to the mill. What would happen if she stopped by there? Would she be welcome?

And would Ole Andersen ever stop by here again, now that he had no reason? Or had all the joy ended with Christmas?

She would like to think of him as a friend. But ach, no, she lied. She would like a chance at something more.

With a sigh, she let herself back into the kitchen and shut the door firmly behind her.

****

Snow came, so much snow it clogged the path between the house and the mill, and Ole had to sweep it three times before he gave up and let it fall. If the past year and a half had taught him anything, it was that sometimes there was no point fighting the inevitable.

Hanne did not seem to notice the forbidding weather. She could not stop talking about Christmas Day, reciting every detail of how it had been and speculating over the possibilities for those who had not shared their wishes.

"What do you think Master Schou will wish for, Papa? Or Mistress Hensen?"

When Ole saw her this way, eyes bright and cheeks flushed with excitement, he could not help but smile.

"I do not know, lamb," he answered patiently every time she asked. "Each to his or her own wish."

He did not point out that all the wishes they'd heard had been for others, rather than the cookie recipient. But he did wonder—what might they have wished, those who had not received a snowdrop?

What was to stop them from wishing, even without the sweetmeat?

Him, for instance. He would wish Hanne would remain always as she was now, a child unburdened by grief. Nothing, nothing for himself, despite his loneliness.

Loneliness was just, well, part of loss. Something with which he'd have to live the rest of his life. He must get used to working with it, sleeping with it. For there could never be another Dorrit.

He reined in his thoughts there, deeming them dangerous, but he could not help wondering for what the alderman's daughter would wish.

Funny, he had known her since he and Dorrit moved here as newlyweds, some eight years ago, known her as the alderman's daughter, that was. He'd seen her in passing and given her the respect of a nod. She'd seemed reserved and, he might have said, a bit snooty.

Not so, not at all. What impressed him most of all was her warmth, and the expression in her eyes when she'd glanced back at all the members of the town following her in a train.

Her smile.

Ah, something else he'd learned. A smile was a priceless thing, fleeting and all too soon gone.

"Papa, what was your favorite part of Christmas Day?"

The smile in Mistress Lissi's eyes.

But he said, "The singing, I think." So spontaneous it had been, and so infectious. As the villagers wound their way from door to door, they'd joined in the old carols, the ones he remembered from his childhood.

Amazing what could come from one act of kindness. And a terrible shame it had to end.

Perhaps it didn't.

In this bad weather, folks shut inside would use a hefty measure of fuel. He'd already given Mistress Lissi most of his surplus to replace what she'd used in her oven. But ach, he was young and strong enough to cut more, ja? And as a kindness, he could make sure his neighbors had enough, perform what act of caring he might.

Starting with the alderman's daughter.

With brutal honesty, he examined the idea, and the contents of his heart. Did he just want to see her? Have an excuse for her to open her kitchen door to him and maybe—maybe greet him with her smile?

Nay, it was a good thing to do. An armload of wood here or there made a small enough thing.

Small as a snowdrop.

"Come, Hanne, let us play a game."

"Papa?" Hanne looked astonished. "Do you not need to go to work in the mill?"

"The mill will remain closed today. The snow demands it."

"I like the snow." Her eyes shone.

"But tomorrow—ja, you shall come to the forest with me, and help me begin a new venture."

"Me, Papa?"

He bopped her on the nose lovingly. "Ja, you shall help me pick up sticks."

She laughed—his beautiful daughter, who had rarely stopped crying this last year, laughed at him. And the bubble of joy once more rose in his chest.

"What game shall we play?"

"One of your choosing, pet."

Joyfully, Hanne took him by the hand.

Chapter Seven

The following Sunday, most everyone met at church. Mitte insisted Lissi wear Mama's bright shawl again, to cheer folk up, so she said. They sat in their old pew at the front, and despite the return of bright sunshine outside, the interior of the building felt cold.

Reverend Pedersen preached a cautious sermon. Indeed, it made Lissi fall to thinking about the state of his soul. Did he, like the rest of them, struggle to find joy?

She had not offered him a wish. A terrible oversight, perhaps. There simply had not been enough.

The church felt not only chilly but empty, even though when Lissi glanced over her shoulder, she saw nearly everyone had come. The miller, his light-brown hair shining in the low light, sat two pews behind her, with his young daughter.

Ach, but Lissi liked his hair. The way it fell across his forehead, over-long, and added to his earnest expression. She liked the strength that lay in his heavy-boned face, and the way that face warmed when he smiled.

She turned forward again in her seat. She had no business numbering the things she liked about the miller.

Only when Reverend Pedersen called upon them to sing a hymn, at the end of the service, did the church come to life. Voices lifted all together as they had on

Christmas morning, and along with them Lissi felt her spirits rise.

Lissi and Mitte were among the last to leave the church after the service. Lissi found Ole and his daughter waiting for her, and she joined them even as Mitte stepped away to speak with the reverend.

Ole gave her a smile. "Mistress Lissi, how are you this day?"

"Well. I am well." After a fleeting look in his eyes, she focused on Hanne instead. "Good morning, Hanne."

Hanne gave her a smile that, except for her missing front teeth, mirrored her father's.

"That was some storm we had, eh?" Ole said, apparently determined to engage Lissi in conversation.

"Indeed. It is a long time since I have seen this much snow."

He fixed her with an earnest gaze. "You have all you need, at your house?"

"I think so."

"Good. Because I believe we should help each other more, ja?"

Ach, so he just wanted to foster a spirit of help in the village. His concern was not aimed at her, specifically. "Of course," she agreed meaninglessly.

Hanne reached up to touch Mama's red shawl. "So pretty."

"Thank you, lamb."

Mitte walked up and nodded at Ole. "Miller."

"Mistress Holst. Come, Hanne, away home now."

"What did he want?" Mitte asked as soon as she and Lissi were alone.

"Just to say hello."

Mitte gave her a sharp look. "Are you certain?"

"Ja, sure."

"He did not ask to see you?"

"He will see me plenty around the village." Lissi directed a hard look of her own at her companion. "I told you, Mitte, he is still grieving for his wife. Pray, leave it be."

For once in her life, Mitte bit her tongue, though she did not appear happy about it.

****

"There, put your hood up. The wind is sharp this morning." Ole tucked Hanne's curls—the same color as his own hair—into her hood.

"Where are we going, Papa?"

"To deliver the first of the wood we gathered. And look." He opened the door. "We will use your sled."

"For me to ride?"

Ole laughed. "That is for the wood to ride, poppet, and we will pull it together." Though he had no doubt she would ride atop the load before the day was done.

"Where shall we go first?"

"I do not know. Where would you like to stop?"

Hanne's face lit. "At Mistress Lissi's house."

Ole's heart leaped. Part of him would like nothing better than to see the alderman's daughter this morning. The rest of him, though, felt guilty about it.

As casually as he could manage, he asked, "Why there?"

"She is nice. And pretty."

That she was, and Ole had no business thinking about it.

Somewhere beneath the snow that blanketed the churchyard, Dorrit still wore his ring. He wondered whether she shared his loneliness. Could the dead feel lonely?

"Tell you what, Hanne. We'll go to our closest neighbors first. That's the Karlsens, and our good friend Mistress Krupp. If we have enough wood on the load, we can stop at Mistress Johansen's."

They set off briskly through the chilly morning, so cold the snow creaked underfoot and their breath came in frosty puffs. To Ole's surprise, others were out and about. When they reached the Karlsens', Holger paused from sweeping his front path to give them a broad smile.

"Good morning, Ole, Hanne. What are you about?"

"Taking this load of wood around to share. Do you need some?"

"Well, that is kind of you." Holger scratched his head. "My sister has enough for now, but I dare say Ebba will need some. She is feeling unwell."

Ole sobered instantly. "Not the sickness?"

"Nay, just the ague, she thinks. But what does one want at such a time, more than to keep snug and warm?"

"We will head there, then."

"Hang on, I will come with you and sweep her path for her. One good turn deserves another, eh?"

After calling to his sister, who came to the door and waved, they set off. "Have you shut up the mill, then?" Holger asked.

"Just for the day. No one has any grain to grind. I thought I would make myself useful, anyway."

"A worthy ambition." Holger's craggy face wrinkled. "Something should be done about it."

"About what?"

"Growing grain enough so folks have their daily bread."

"Ja, but there aren't enough hands left to work the

fields."

"Let me give it some thought."

They stopped at the home of Ebba Krupp, who opened the door to them wrapped in a blanket. Her eyes lit when Ole explained their mission.

"Ach, that would be useful. I would dearly love to make myself a warm drink this morning."

They filled her kitchen woodbox, Hanne helping to carry an armful of sticks at a time, while Holger cleared the path outside.

Before they left, Ole told the older woman, "You must ask me if you need anything. You help to watch Hanne. I will help you in turn."

Ebba's eyes sparkled with tears. "It has been so hard. Each of us has been hoeing his own row."

"Ja, but that can change."

As they left, Holger began singing a song in his deep baritone—one of the Christmas hymns from the other day—and Hanne joined in, her voice like a bird's. Ole did not sing, but his gaze fixed on the alderman's house, and his heart beat faster.

"What is this? Carolers?" Mitte demanded when she hauled open the kitchen door.

Holger gave her his big grin. "We are spreading good cheer," he announced. "I will sweep your walk while Ole and Hanne fill your woodbox."

"Well, is that not neighborly?" Mitte stepped aside, and Ole saw Lissi working beside the kitchen fire. A smile came to his face, one he could not hold back.

"Good morning, mistress."

"Good morning, Master Ole and Hanne. What is all this?"

"We have come to fill your woodbox, as you see."

"Just like elves!" She laughed, and the very air of the kitchen seemed to warm and brighten. She bent to tell Hanne, "You are a very pretty elf, indeed. And a fine helper for your papa."

Mitte said, "You are setting that child a fine example, Ole Andersen. With so few of us left, we should be helping one another each and every day."

"Ja." Lissi wrapped her arms around herself. "I wish I could do more."

Ole allowed himself the pleasure of examining her face, from golden curls to rounded chin. "You? You started it all, I am thinking, with your gifts of wishes."

Hanne spoke up. "Mistress Lissi, do we need to have a magic cookie in order to make a wish?"

Lissi bent to her once more. "No, to be sure, poppet. You can make a wish anytime."

"And will it come true?"

"Well, that is the question. The snowdrops made it easy to believe, ja? And the secret is all in believing. I suspect any wish you make, for good, and that you believe in with your whole heart, can come true."

"So, even the people who did not get cookies can have wishes?"

"Why, certainly, angel."

"Then Papa can have a wish. And you may."

Lissi shot a startled look at Ole. "So we might."

Earnestly, Hanne asked, "Can I do the believing for other people?"

Lissi's gaze softened. "I am very afraid not, Hanne. Each heart must believe for itself."

Chapter Eight

Thereafter, good deeds spread through the village the way the sickness once had, but with far more fortunate effect. Even though, in the days that followed, winter closed its cold fist around Gjerhold, folk no longer shut themselves away in their houses. Lissi had only to glance outside to see a neighbor setting off purposefully on some errand, or standing at another's gate.

The very mood of the place had changed. Ole Andersen making his rounds delivering firewood became a regular event, a pied piper sort of affair, accompanied by others offering their services. Holger cleared paths, others tended stock or merely stopped in to chat with those fallen victim to the winter grippe.

One Sunday, Reverend Pedersen spoke of it. The old preacher seemed far less sunk in gloom, and his words rose through the cold air inside the church on little currents of hope.

After, Mitte invited him back to dinner, and Lissi could only wonder at the looks that passed between the two. Love in the air here, in Gjerhold?

Why not? And why not for Reverend Pedersen and Mitte, though a more unlikely pair Lissi could scarcely imagine. Mama used to say no one was too old or too young for love.

And, Lissi wanted to see Mitte happy, more than anything.

They weren't the only ones, to Lissi's surprise. As she made her way around the village, she saw a number of seemingly unlikely pairings. Those left alone, and lonely, bringing comfort to neighbors.

Bonding together, maybe.

It made Lissi ache inside, though in a good way. She ached also to see Ole Andersen. Just to lay eyes on him satisfied her in ways she could not describe. The fall of that light brown hair over his forehead... Ach, the man needed a haircut in the worst way, though it would be a crime against God and nature to shear such locks.

And she wanted to see the smile take hold in those grave eyes of his. Ole Andersen smiled first with his eyes, so he did. A rare and wonderful thing.

She awoke in the morning thinking of him, and his face became the last in her mind at night.

She questioned herself over it ceaselessly. She couldn't be losing her heart to the miller. Could she?

Disastrous. For though he still came by with loads of firewood every other day or so, and though he gave her his smile, it had gone no further. He'd not spoken of seeing her again.

He still loved his wife.

Foolish as she was, Lissi made a wish about it, believing—believing hard, the way she'd told Hanne. It was all about the believing.

The next day, Thora Hensen came to see her.

Thora was the spinster who had donated the sugar meant for her wedding cake, to dust the Christmas snowdrops. Already past the accepted marrying age when she'd planned to wed—as was Lissi now—she'd lost her intended to the black death.

She came to Lissi's door with a parcel in her arms,

which she lost no time in unwrapping, once inside.

"I have been going through a few things," Thora announced. "There's just me alone in that house now, to feed and clothe. I don't need much."

Lissi looked at her sympathetically. Thora appeared older than her years, her eyes tired.

"Since Christmas," she went on, "I have been thinking. You know I once was a fairly good seamstress. I made this."

She unfolded a garment from the parcel, a gown of white. Embroidered all over with tiny stitches, it could be only one thing.

"That's your wedding dress."

A wistful look came to Thora's face. "Ja. The hours I worked over this, waiting for Per to come home. He never did, and died in Flanders. Did you know that?"

"Ja," Lissi said softly.

"For weeks and months I wept, wishing I might die too. But the Death did not take me." She met Lissi's gaze. "Do you know why it took some, and not others?"

Lissi shook her head. She'd wondered about that too, but had no answer. "Even here under this roof, it was so."

"The will of God, perhaps. No matter. I was living and yet was not, until Christmas when you gave me that cookie, and a wish. I'll not tell you what I wished for. But I wondered if you might have a use for this."

"The dress? Me? Nay."

"I thought, as I have so much in clothing I will never use again, and some yardages of cloth also, I might pass the things out in the village. This dress made me think of you. It would fit, I suppose."

"No doubt. But why would I have need of a wedding

dress?"

Thora shrugged. "Not many of us left are of an age for marrying. Take it. Put it away. It will gladden my heart."

Perhaps, Lissi thought, Thora merely wanted rid of the garment because it brought her sorrow. She nodded. "If you wish."

"Lissi, we must return to a time of hope. And new beginnings. We have kept ourselves, and our hearts, shut away far too long."

"I agree. Thank you, Thora. It is a beautiful dress."

"Ja, and meant for beautiful occasions, not to be crushed into a trunk."

"It is a good idea you have. I too have clothing packed away here, of Mama's and Papa's. People can use the things, especially the warm garments during the cold."

"Ja. Can you sew?"

"I can."

"If you discover a particular need, let me know. As I say, I have some good woolen fabric. We could work together and make what's needed."

Lissi smiled. "I would like that very much."

"And bless you, Lissi Johansen, for your snowdrop cookies. They made a difference."

Thora turned to the door, before hesitating. "Ach, and the next time you see the miller, take a look at his coat." She quirked an eyebrow. "Looks to me like he could use a better one."

****

Lissi cracked the lid of the trunk and the smell of the garments inside assailed her. In an instant, she was with Mama again, watching her fold fresh lavender between the layers of cloth. With such care and love had Mama done everything.

The last hands to touch these garments had been hers.

"The moth does not like the scent of lavender, girls. And we do not like the moth."

Ach, the sweetness of Mama's voice in her ear again. Gone, gone just like Dagny. For an instant, grief assailed Lissi, so deep it felt insupportable. She wanted to bow her head and weep into the trunk.

But what good would that do anyone?

Instead she shook out the stored garments, one by one. Anything she or Mitte could not use should be given to those who could, and there were some fine things.

A christening shawl used for both her and Dagny. She laid that aside. A woolen dress, out of fashion. Ach, but what was fashion, when it came to the cold?

And…what was this?

Tiny bits of dried lavender fell when she shook out the garment. An embroidered shawl, red like Mama's that Lissi had worn at Christmas. But made for a child. This had been Dagny's. Both of them had owned small versions, but Lissi's had gotten torn.

Mama had packed this one away. Why? Because it was made with love, and thus valuable to her.

Lissi smoothed her fingers over the bright embroidery, and a vision of Hanne Andersen swam before her eyes. This was meant for Hanne. Lissi wanted to go at once and give it to the child.

She bit her lip. She'd been doing her best to avoid the miller, mainly because of the way it felt being with him—at once wonderful and painfully bittersweet. But she could not allow herself to be selfish about it.

The next garment she drew from the trunk proved to be Papa's coat. Sewn from stout cloth, it was thick and warm, very fine indeed.

And would no doubt fit the miller.

She smoothed both garments over her arm and got to her feet.

There was no time like the present to take these to the Andersens.

Chapter Nine

Lissi did not find the miller at home. A lazy plume of smoke wafted up from his chimney, proving he had been there not long since, but both house and mill stood closed.

Following footprints in the new-fallen snow, Lissi soon heard the ringing of an axe in the woodland beyond. Softly she approached and took in the scene.

Ole Andersen swung his axe with controlled power and determination. A competent woodsman, despite that being something other than his first calling.

Hanne, keeping well out of his way, collected sticks and branches, and dragged them to a nearby sled. She it was who caught sight of Lissi and cried, "Papa?"

Ole lowered his axe. Lissi had—let it be admitted—pawed through her mama's trunk and walked far just for an excuse to see him smile, but his stare looked level and grave.

He eased his stance and touched his hat. "Mistress? You are in need of something?"

Your laughter. Your conversation. Time spent with you, only that.

She said, "I did not mean to interrupt your work."

"It is fine. The sled is nearly full, and we will be heading back to the house soon."

"What is that?" Blue eyes round, Hanne tiptoed up and touched Dagny's shawl, which lay uppermost over

Lissi's arm.

"It is something I am hoping you can use."

"Me?"

"Ja." Lissi shook it out. "It is very like the one I wore at Christmas, that you admired so much. That one belonged to my mama. This one belonged to my sister, Dagny, when she was your age. I found it while going through some things this morning. Would you like to have it?"

"Me?" Hanne squeaked again.

"Ah, now," Ole said, straightening his spine. "Are you certain you want to give that away, Mistress Lissi?"

"Certain, ja."

"It is precious."

"Dagny certainly cannot wear it again. But I thought it might bring Hanne some happiness." She smiled at the girl. "Hanne is precious, also."

Hanne shot a look of longing at her father but said nothing. Would Ole's pride cause him to refuse the gift?

"Besides," Lissi urged, "Hanne has been working very hard helping supply fuel to our neighbors. She deserves a reward."

"We do not help others for reward." But Lissi could tell Ole's battle was lost, his gaze gone soft upon his daughter's face.

"Very true," Lissi said softly. "But if it will gladden Hanne's heart—"

"Ja, thank you, Mistress Lissi. It is very kind of you. Hanne, you may have the shawl."

"*Tak*, Mistress Lissi," Hanne said, needing no further urging.

"Here, let us put it on you. Over your cloak, for now, I think, since it is so very cold."

Hanne stood perfectly still while Lissi wrapped her in the bright shawl. Lissi, surprised at how right it felt having her arms around the child, had to clear her throat before she spoke again. "There you are."

"Papa, am I beautiful?"

"So beautiful." Ole's smile came at last, but it looked wistful.

"As beautiful as Mistress Lissi?"

"Well, now. Ja—so I think. That shawl is every bit as beautiful as hers."

"May I go and show it to Mistress Krupp?"

"Ja, go."

Hanne pelted off, kicking up snow behind her—a child, after all. Lissi and Ole looked at one another.

She said "I hope you do not mind the gift."

"It was very kind."

"I have something else here. It belonged to my father. A good, stout coat, warm and almost new when he d-died." Lissi approached him and held out the garment. "I think it will fit you and—it would give me great gladness if you would accept it."

There. Let his pride get around that! It wanted to. She saw it flash in his eyes before they fixed on Papa's coat.

"Are you certain?" he asked again. "There are others in Gjerhold who might need it more."

"Those others are not out in the cold, cutting and gathering fuel for the rest of the village. You are my first choice. If you do not want the coat, I will give it to someone else."

"I did not say I do not want it."

"You spend most of the day out here in all weather. I worry—" In the act of holding the coat up to him, to make sure it would fit, she froze.

Their eyes met, and Ole swallowed hard. "You worry—for me?"

"Ja. And this coat, it was just lying in the trunk, doing good for no one."

Ole dropped his axe and his hands came up to cover hers. So seldom had he touched her, and so dearly had she longed for it, warmth kindled and rushed through her.

What would he do if she took a step forward into his arms? Back away in horror? What, if she pressed her lips to his? Would his lips feel cold? Or as warm as he made her feel?

Before she could deny the impulse, she lifted onto her toes—Ole Andersen was very tall—and followed thought with deed.

Warm. Despite the chilly air, the kiss felt very warm. His lips seemed surprisingly supple. After a shocked moment, they softened and welcomed hers. His hands tightened on her fingers, and drew her closer.

The kiss, precious and fragile, lasted but a moment, long enough to persuade Lissi of two things. She'd never dreamed of such happiness as might be found in Ole Andersen's arms, and, ja, she was losing her heart to this man.

Ach, how could she let it happen? She'd been so careful of her heart, for so long. And he—he might not welcome a second love.

That became very clear as he released her hands and stepped away, staring at Lissi with a combination of doubt and consternation.

"Mistress, I apologize. I do not know what came over me."

Ja, a gentleman was Ole Andersen, who would take blame even though the kiss had been all Lissi's doing.

Her heart thudded in her breast, and a score of things she might say plowed through her head. *What is a kiss between friends? Are we not friends? It was but a kiss...*

She said none of them. It had not been but a kiss, and she felt far too shaken for blithe statements. Instead, grief touched her. So long had she taken, to find the man who might claim her heart. And here he stood, still in love with someone else.

What to do about it? Was there anything she could do? She wondered, as they followed in Hanne's wake, Ole pulling the loaded sled.

She could throw herself at him—again. Speak honestly, since he seemed an honest man. But if she admitted her feelings and he did not—could not—return them, how humiliating that would be. And she had to see him almost every day.

It started snowing as they walked home, tiny flakes that swirled and danced like icing sugar and made the air feel colder. Lissi didn't mind. The memory of Ole's kiss helped keep her warm.

Chapter Ten

She had kissed him. There, in the woodland, with the smell of pine all around, and the birds calling from the tops of the trees, Lissi had. Relive it as he might, Ole could put no other interpretation upon the occurrence.

And relive it he did. During the following afternoon and, let it be admitted, night time, he experienced those moments over and over and over again, with all their accompanying sensations.

Warmth. Wonder. A surprising amount of passion, though he shouldn't be surprised, Lissi being a beautiful young woman.

Guilt.

The guilt snuck in the back door of his pleasure, the way a vicious wolf might, there every time he turned around. It nipped at his ankles and drew blood.

What, after all, was a single kiss from a friend? She had been stirred by gifting him with her father's coat. They had so little to give these days. And he—

He had a wife less than a year in the ground. How could he so betray her, and find pleasure in another woman's kiss?

He had found pleasure, though, and needed to admit it. Just as, in all honesty, he should admit he longed to kiss Lissi Johansen again.

There lay the danger. A simple kiss on the cheek—or, ja, the lips—was one thing. He found he wanted far more.

Well, he was a man, wasn't he? Lonely in his bed, and in his life. And the alderman's daughter was beautiful, if in a far different way than his Dorrit.

It did not seem to matter to the blood pumping through his veins, or the desire in his heart. He had to be careful. A lovely thing had been born here in Gjerhold, a spirit of sharing and giving, and helping one another.

He might spoil that so easily by following impulses he had no right to own.

He arose that next morning, having slept precious little, and crept across the cold plank floor to peer at himself in the water of the wash basin. He remembered Dorrit grooming her hair in front of this basin, combing out the strands like pale butter and braiding them. And him, Ole, watching all the while, aching at how lovely she was. She had no longer looked like that the last time he saw her, when he put her in the ground—skin darkened by the terrible buboes, eyes widened with remembered agony.

His very spirit shied from that image. He should have told her he loved her despite her changed appearance, but he hadn't. He'd been too shocked and worn with nursing both her and Rikke, losing Rikke and burying her ahead of her mother, praying all the while Hanne would be all right.

"I still love you," he whispered now. How dared he think about kissing another woman? Kissing her, and caressing her soft skin?

He had promised Dorrit he would take care of Hanne, and that he would do. Going forward, it must all be about his daughter. Not the alderman's.

He turned away from the basin, and his eyes fell on

the coat, laid across the back of a chair. Lissi had wanted him to try it on before she left yesterday. He'd found every excuse not to. Now he ran his calloused palm across the garment. The finest wool it was, thick and warm, better than he deserved. He would only spoil it, while performing his chores.

On impulse, though, he donned the coat over his nightshirt. It sat on his shoulders and eased around him, the perfect fit.

How had Lissi known? Had she measured the breadth of his shoulders, the length of his arms, with her gaze?

Was it possible she wanted him, as much as he wanted her?

He tossed his head, flinging the brown hair out of his eyes. Nay, and nay. She was merely a kind woman. Quite possibly the kindest he'd ever known.

****

"I will not be at home for supper tonight." Mitte announced it blithely as she and Lissi sorted through the linens. "I will be taking supper with Reverend Pedersen."

"Oh?" Lissi quirked an eyebrow at her old friend. "How did this come about?"

"He asked me." A dull flush suffused Mitte's cheeks, an occurrence so rare it made Lissi stare. "You know I have been advising him about keeping the church open."

Haranguing him, more likely.

"Well, we are going to discuss that. And share a meal. And, perhaps, something more."

"Mitte!"

"Do not look so shocked, girl. The reverend is a fine man, if a bit wanting in direction at the moment. He lost his wife, you know. Who could blame him for closing his doors and hiding? But me, I am the woman for giving direction."

"Indeed."

"You know, I think there is something in the air of this village, these days since Christmas. People are joining together, helping one another. Not just me and Josef."

Josef.

"But Arne Karlsen and Solveig Svensen as well."

"Never!"

"Why not? They are both widowed and lonely. And there is you and the miller."

"There is no hope for me and the miller." Even though Lissi could still feel his lips on hers, warm and tender. And even though her heart ached for his company, the gentle comfort of it, the sense of belonging.

All folk wished to belong with someone, that was true.

"Ole—"

"Is still in love with his wife. Ja, you keep telling me that. Dorrit was a fine woman, worthy of his love."

Lissi's heart sank.

"But she is gone, and you are here. He needs to get that through his wooden head. Men can be thick, ja—the miller, it seems, especially so."

Distressed, Lissi said nothing. What if Mitte and the reverend came to an understanding? What if he asked this woman—the last remaining member of Lissi's family—to marry him?

Lissi would be left all alone in this big house. She didn't think she could bear it.

"It must have been those cookies," Mitte decided.

"Oh?"

"All those wishes flying around the village, folk giving theirs away to one another. People are lonely. You should be happy the magic held."

"I am happy."

"You do not look it." Mitte turned to Lissi and gazed at her, suddenly serious. "I tell you, Lissi, if you want something, wish for it, and wish hard. You do not need a cookie to make it happen. What is it you told everyone else on Christmas? You just need to believe."

"Ja, Mitte." Lissi leaned forward and hugged her old nurse. Mitte's arms closed around her with a fierce love she rarely expressed.

Mitte whispered, "If I had a wish, girl, I'd wish for your happiness."

"Ach?" Lissi drew away. "I thought you'd wish for the good reverend's favor."

"I shall have that anyway. Just you wait and see."

Chapter Eleven

"I have been thinking," Arne Karlsen said to Ole as he placed an armload of firewood on Ole's sled. Arne had volunteered to come help in the woodland, and had brought his own sleigh—to make the task go quicker, he said.

Ole would not argue. Arne might be in his fifties but was still a strapping man, well suited to the task.

Ole had heard just today, from Ebba, of all people, that Arne had been paying calls on the widow Svensen. It had surprised Ole, even though it shouldn't.

Now Arne went on. "Given this spirit of cooperation that has been fostered since Christmas, you cutting wood, my brother sweeping everyone's paths, and the rest of us tending one another's stock, I say we should extend it."

"How so?" Ole paused and shivered a bit in the chilly air. He still wore his old, tattered coat, lacking the nerve to wear the new one.

"Well." Arne leaned on a branch. "Last year's harvest was a failure, good as."

"Ja."

"The village is paying for it now. Bellies are empty, and your grinding wheel is mostly idle. But spring will come again. I tell you, Ole…" Arne lifted bushy eyebrows. "Spring always comes. Just like the snowdrops, eh?" He laughed, showing craggy teeth.

"I suppose so."

"There are not so many of us left here in Gjerhold. Not enough to work all the farms. But what if we banded together as we have been doing and farmed one or two? All worked the land, and all shared the harvest when it comes."

Ole tried to look that far ahead, through the long winter, the sweetness of spring, and to the summer ripe with grain. It was hard to do.

But he said, "A fine idea, Arne."

"If I organize the others, will you join in?"

"I am no farmer."

"No matter. You are good with an axe. Why not a hoe? It will keep your mill grinding grain."

"Ja. Count me in."

Arne grinned and tossed his head. "I don't know about you, but I am ready to take a step away from the dark time, out of the grief. Even if that means starting over. And, damn it, I don't care so much about the bread. But I want enough grain to brew some ale!"

****

Wishes, so Lissi decided after her conversation with Mitte, were perilous things. Ach, it was all well and good passing them out to others, encouraging them to make their choices. Another thing entirely, making them for oneself.

So much room for error. No chance, often, of going back again. Now that she looked at it, wishing felt very much like leaping off a cliff.

Blindfolded.

She needed to believe she would not smash on the rocks below. Or lose her heart.

But quite possibly, she reflected as she straightened

up the house and sorted through a few more garments that afternoon, her heart was already lost. For she could not stop thinking about Ole Andersen, not when she got up in the morning and went about her chores. Not when she awoke in the night. She felt his lips on hers again and saw the gentle, steady light burning in his gray eyes.

What eyes the man had! Lissi would wager she glimpsed his soul there.

It was beautiful.

"What are you up to, today?" Mitte asked as she went out the door, bound for Reverend Pedersen's house. She would whip that man into shape, whether he liked it or not. Lissi rather suspected he would like it.

"I thought I would take some of these things to Solveig, since they might fit her old father."

"A considerate impulse. And that yellow gown?"

"I thought Solveig herself might use it."

Mitte snorted. "What of Hanne Andersen?"

"What of her?"

"I doubt that child can remember the last time she had a new dress. And it will look much better on her than on old Solveig."

"Hanne already got the shawl." Lissi bit her lips. "I do not want to play favorites."

"Even if you might have them? Take the gown to the miller's. It can be cut down for Hanne."

Lissi nodded and followed Mitte out. The old woman went off toward the church. Lissi took the other path.

Another clear, cold day, fast brightening upon last night's fresh dusting of snow. Blue sky showed in patches, and the ground glistened.

A perfect day for wishing.

What if Lissi wished as she went? What if, with every step, she prayed the miller might be in this afternoon, that he would listen to all she had to say. That she might find the courage to speak plainly to him, as an honest woman should, to the man she—

Loved.

Ach, and what if she spoiled everything? Their casual friendship, her connection with little Hanne, the quiet joy she found in their company?

She had to believe—believe honesty would spoil nothing. Believe in the wish that now possessed her heart.

She knocked at Ole's house door, which sorely needed painting, and waited, fearful that despite all her hoping he would not be home.

He opened the door with the brown hair tumbling over his forehead and flour on his hands. For one blinding instant, she thought he looked glad to see her. Then he blinked, and she saw only courtesy in his eyes.

"Mistress Lissi?"

"Lissi. Surely you can call me that, since we are friends?" Lissi could not keep her gaze from his lips, while the ache increased inside.

"Ja, of course. Please to come in." He backed from the door, holding up his hands. "You caught me in the middle of baking bread for Hanne's supper. You would think I would be good with flour, eh? But, nay. It is something I have struggled with since—" He paused abruptly and ended with, "Dorrit turned out a grand loaf."

"Is Hanne not here?"

"Nay, she has gone to see Ebba, who still feels under the weather." At Lissi's startled look, he quickly added,

"Not the sickness. Just the grippe."

"It is the time of year for it." Whoever would have thought a pronouncement of common illness would bring relief?

Lissi eyed the mess of dough on the table and removed her cloak. "Let me help."

"I cannot ask—"

"You are not asking. I have offered." Lissi pushed up her sleeves and went to the table. "You certainly cannot afford to waste the flour."

"That is so. This is not first quality, as it is. But the girl must be fed."

Lissi, vigorously kneading the bread on the floury table, met his gaze. "And you, Ole? What do you need?"

He shrugged.

"You must also be fed. Cared for." Lissi sucked in a breath. "Loved."

There—she'd said it. Would he take the word as meant?

Something flickered in his eyes, light—and darkness.

He said nothing, and Lissi's heart cramped in her chest.

"You remember"—Lissi thumped the dough— "Hanne's wish for you on Christmas morning. Hanne would not mind, should you, could you find happiness again."

"Ja, I know. It is not Hanne."

"Dorrit." Lissi spoke the name of his dead wife, and her heart finished coming apart in her breast. "Was she the sort of woman to deny you happiness?"

"Not she, nay."

"Who, then?"

He leaned toward her, put out one finger, and laid it beneath her chin, turning her face toward him.

"You are a good woman, Lissi Johansen, with a kind heart. And so…so beautiful—"

His gaze met hers, and whatever other words he meant to say died. Instead of speaking them, he bent his head and laid his lips gently on hers.

Lissi's hands stilled in the dough, and her heart leaped like a salmon in the spring. Ach, so wishes did come true.

Eyes closed, she let herself be kissed, a glorious thing. Warm and soft it was, and magically persuasive. When Ole urged her lips apart, she abandoned her task and moved into his arms. Twining her arms around his neck, she gave herself to the kiss, gave her heart to him right there in his kitchen.

Far too soon—long before she wanted it—he ended the kiss and rested his forehead against hers. She could feel the warmth of him and the double-time pounding of his heart.

What would he do if she kissed him again?

Before she could decide, he brushed her hair back from her face, his touch tender. How could a man with such big, strong hands be so gentle? It made her knees go weak.

She felt him gather himself, stiffen his resolve before he said, "I apologize. I should not have done that."

"Nay?" The word trembled from her.

"You have been good to Hanne, and to me. I have no right to—to complicate things."

Lissi closed her eyes on a wave of pain. Ja, he had given in to a moment's temptation. Now he regretted it. This was how he let her know he was not ready to care for another woman.

Tell him, her heart urged. *Say it out plain, that you want a life with him. That you want to forsake all others, to be here in his home with him. In his bed, in his life.*

And, she countered her heart, *have him throw it back in my face?*

"I have got flour all over your shirt." Removing her hands from where they still curled around his neck, she took a step backward.

"It does not matter."

"Let me help you shape that loaf, so I may be on my way."

Hastily, she turned back to the table, blinking fiercely so he wouldn't see the tears in her eyes. "I have been busy sorting through my parents' and Dagny's things. I have some garments to take to Solveig, and that yellow gown you see there. I thought it might be cut down for Hanne. Well, Mitte thought so."

She stopped speaking, aware her tongue tripped over itself.

"You are very kind, Lissi. Lissi, please look at me."

"I am almost done here, and then you can set the loaf to rise—"

"Lissi, the last thing I wish to do is hurt your feelings."

He was as bad at that as at shaping a loaf. But Lissi forgave him. She would forgive this man anything.

Ach, curse wishing, anyway. All it did was raise your hopes so they came crashing down.

Somehow, she found the courage to look at him. "Ole, do not worry. I understand. Grief is grief."

He drew a breath that expanded his chest. "I am— well, attracted to you. That must be plain. But—"

"But I am not Dorrit."

He blinked as if she'd struck him across the face. "Not that. I am not ready—"

He did not love her. Not as she loved him. For if he did, his heart would leap to it, just as hers had.

He would not be able to hold it back.

The tears in her eyes blurred him where he stood. "I must go. Let the loaf rise—"

"I know."

"It should bake in time for Hanne's supper."

"Lissi, I am sorry—"

Not letting him finish, she fled. But ja, she left the pieces of her heart behind.

Chapter Twelve

"It will do no good, moping," Mitte told Lissi later that same evening. "You know what your mama used to say. It is better to stay busy than to moan and weep."

"I am not weeping. Or moaning," Lissi retorted.

"Work keeps the mind occupied, and it can accomplish a great deal, besides."

Lissi, slumped in a chair, looked up at her old nurse. "It is you who said that, not Mama."

"She learned it from me." Mitte's expression softened. "Why do you grieve? Is it the miller?"

Far too humiliated for anything but honesty, Lissi admitted, "I love him, Mitte. And he does not want me. He doesn't want my heart."

"Ah." Mitte pulled a stool up to Lissi's side and took her hand. "The man must be a fool. Your heart, my girl, is a rare and precious gift."

"One he cannot accept."

Mitte put her head on one side. "A hard thing to bear, especially for you."

"Eh?"

"It has taken you overlong to bestow the gift of your heart. In fact, I feared it might never happen. It makes you fierce in your love. But, my girl, look what you have endured this past year or more. You can endure this also."

"Maybe I cannot. Perhaps this will be the thing to

break me."

"Never."

"He kissed me, Mitte. And it was—" But Lissi had no words.

"If he kissed you, what is he about, handing you back your heart?"

"I am not enough for him. I am not Dorrit."

"Now, you banish that thought right out of your head, girl. Not good enough for the miller?" Mitte snorted. "Stupid man."

"He wants her back, I think."

"Of course he does. We want all of them back. We ache for it. But we cannot have that, can we? And if Christmas made one thing clear, it is that we need to go on."

Lissi met the old woman's eyes. "Christmas?"

"All that wishing. All that hope. It's like shutting a beautiful bird inside a box."

"Eh?"

"When you open the box, that bird is going to fly out, and you will not get it back in. Because it wants to fly.

"Or it is like those snowdrops." Mitte stroked Lissi's hair. "They come up in the spring, sometimes far too early. When the snow falls upon them, what do they do? Do they pull their heads back into the dark soil? Nay, they stand there, brave, and believe the warmth will come."

Tears flooded Lissi's eyes.

"Do not try to shut your bird in the box, Lissi. She has to fly. We all *need* to love. Even if those first flights hurt."

Lissi nodded.

Mitte said, more briskly, returning to her ordinary manner, "Which is why I am off to see the good reverend. That man is going to marry me, whether he knows it or not."

She went out, and the thoughts teemed in Lissi's mind. Mitte, to wed? She'd been a spinster since long before Lissi could remember. And wed, would she go off to live at the tiny vicarage? That would indeed leave Lissi all alone here in this house, once so full of bustle and laughter.

Another thing she could not bear.

Looking back on the past months, it seemed she saw a terrible string of events she could not bear. Yet had.

Perhaps she was stronger than she knew. Strong enough to forfeit Ole's love, until he felt ready to share his life, again? If he ever did.

But it was not past wishing, that Ole might open the box that held his happiness, and release it to fly with her own.

****

The first thing Ole heard when he stepped out of his house the next morning was laughter.

The sound stopped him where he stood, his boots in the newly fallen snow he'd come out to sweep. It had been so long since he'd heard such a thing, ringing through the clear, still air, it felt like stepping into sunlight from darkness.

Ja, he thought as he employed his broom on the path. The alderman's daughter had started something with her gifts of cookies and wishes. Folk were—well, different. They sought out one another for conversation and, ja, laughter, just like two of his neighbors now speaking across the wattle fence. They lent a hand. They shared.

There must be some magic in it.

Such a simple thing for Lissi Johansen to do. A basket full of cookies made from gleaned ingredients, to accomplish so much.

She had wisdom. Maybe even some magic of her own.

An image of her face rose before his mind's eye. Beautiful blue eyes. Well, it wasn't the color of her eyes that made them beautiful, but the fact that they held understanding. They held compassion. They showed the depths of her spirit, her heart.

His own heart quivered in his chest. He never should have kissed her. Never, if he didn't mean to offer her something more than friendship. For now he feared he'd hurt her feelings—the last thing he ever wished to do.

She deserved a man capable of devotion. But that was him, Ole, wasn't it? He was still devoted to his Dorrit. Part of him always would be. Could he offer Lissi less than all?

Nay, nay.

She deserved a man who would throw himself at her feet. Or no, no. One who would walk beside her, standing tall, his shoulders straight.

Him, again? Ach, but he did not know.

He never should have kissed her. For now he wanted her, day and night. A fine state for a man who possessed only half a heart.

"Papa? What are you doing, just standing there in the snow?"

"Ach, Hanne, do not stand there either, in your nightdress. It is cold. Go get dressed."

"Are we going to the forest today?"

"To the forest, ja."

Hanne ran off, contented. She liked their days spent working together. Indeed, he'd never spent so much time with her in the past, when he worked at the mill.

Things had changed. Perhaps not all for the worse.

The snow crackled underfoot as they walked into the trees, the runners of Hanne's sled shushing behind them. The trip took longer and longer each time, as they cleared the deadfall and moved on.

They passed the place where Lissi had kissed him. Ja, she had kissed him that first time. The magic of the moment still lingered beneath the trees.

For the first time in months, he spoke to his dead wife, in his mind. *Would it be so wrong, Dorrit? Would it be so much a betrayal, to cure the loneliness?*

A single leaf drifted down and touched his shoulder. An answer? He didn't think so.

Yet he continued to speak to Dorrit as he trudged on. He spoke softly, as he used to do when he cradled her in his arms in their bed, at night.

You know I will always love you. When you and I stood before the minister in Middholm, and I spoke the words, that was forever. But, Dorrit, it is like this—I do not believe I can bear a life lived alone.

Widows and widowers remarried. It happened all the time. Oftentimes, he suspected it was a practical arrangement. A homestead needed to be kept, the work shared. Children needed raising. Love was not always involved.

Survival. It was about that.

They were all survivors, those left here in Gjerhold. He did not ask for love. Yet he wanted it—if not for himself, then for Lissi.

A woman like that, all warmth and generosity,

deserved more than he could give. Her very kiss asked for it.

"Here, Papa?"

"Ja, Hanne, we will work here today."

It felt good, plying the axe. He liked the way his blows rang through the chilly air, and the burn of his muscles coming awake.

Such a simple and satisfying thing, bringing the body to life. If only it also worked for the heart.

They labored all the morning long, he breaking up the fallen trees and Hanne gathering them on the sled.

"Papa, I am hungry."

And no doubt cold, too. "Ja, Hanne. You run ahead and stir up the fire. I will bring the sled."

Hanne pelted off ahead of him, and Ole spoke again to Dorrit, in his mind. *You would be so proud of her. Such a good girl. She has strength, this child of ours.* He smiled. *You will never believe what she wished for, at Christmas. Not a doll or a new dress or any of those things. My happiness. Mine.*

Abruptly, he stopped walking, the runners shushing to a halt behind him. Ahead he could see his house and the mill beyond. He could also see the church with its quiet graveyard, all covered in snow.

Without further hesitation, he abandoned the sled and walked on.

Chapter Thirteen

No one had swept the path to the graveyard. Those who lay there slept beneath an unbroken dusting of snow, fallen last night. As Ole went, his big boots made the only tracks.

He knew where they lay, these pieces of his heart, even though there were no markers. No one had time or energy for markers when so many died. It hadn't mattered, then.

How long had it been since he'd come here? For a while, he'd made the walk every day. It must be weeks since he'd directed his feet to this hallowed ground.

But today, he needed to talk to his wife. Nay, that was not right. He'd been talking to her all morning. Now, he needed to hear what she had to say.

The last time he'd seen her, held her in his arms, she'd been in agony, crying out for relief. Wishing for death. It had come as a mercy, and he loved her so much, so much he hadn't thought about the devastation her going would wreak upon his heart.

That was what it meant to love—caring more for the other person than oneself.

After all that, after watching the light fade from her eyes, could he betray her by giving his heart to another? Was he selfish in wishing an end to his loneliness?

He reached the place where she and little Rikke lay, clasped his mittened hands together, and bent his head.

Suddenly, a bright image of Dorrit arose in his mind—not as she'd been at the end, but the hardworking, serene woman with whom he'd lived and striven to build a life.

Ole Andersen, how big is your heart?

His whole body jerked in shock. He'd come here for an answer, ja, but—

The man I knew and loved had a great and mighty heart.

"My heart is shattered, Dorrit. You took the better part of it away with you."

Ole, do you believe in magic?

Ole thought of the alderman's daughter, and her wishes. "Ja."

Remember when Hanne was born? You told me you never knew you could love someone so much.

"I remember."

Then Rikke came along and you loved her just as much. Did that love take anything away from Hanne? Did you have to divide your love up like a measure of flour? Or did the magic of love allow your heart to expand, and love more?

"Ach, Dorrit." Ole's eyes filled with tears.

You wish an answer from me? Drop to your knees.

He did, right there upon her grave. His tears fell into the snow as he reached out with mittened hands—mittens she had knitted for him—and smoothed the snow from her grave, just the way he used to smooth her hair.

He had to blink away the tears, in order to believe what he saw.

There, amid the stubble of dead grass—one tiny snowdrop grew.

All the breath left his body as if he'd been thumped in the chest. Tenderly, most tenderly, he brushed the snow away from all sides.

Impossible. Snowdrops did not come up until spring.

Unless—unless one wished for it. And believed.

Shedding his mittens, he bent to the tiny flower, its head still tucked well down, barely above the soil. New and tender, it had just begun to unfurl.

Like what grew in his heart.

Carefully, he plucked the flower, his fingers nearly too big and clumsy for the task. Then he got to his feet and followed his own path back through the snow.

****

Lissi worked alone in the house, keeping busy, when the knock sounded at the door. By midafternoon, with Mitte once more away to see Reverend Pedersen, the room felt cold, despite the fire. Already, outside, the winter dark descended.

More snow soon, she told herself as she laid aside the cloth for scrubbing the table.

Ach, and who could be at the door? She hauled it open to reveal the tall form of Ole Andersen. He wore his old boots, his hat and mittens.

And her father's coat.

How well it suited him, the color bringing out the gray of his eyes, the rich fleck lending a certain dignity. Or perhaps that came from the way he held himself.

She had not expected to see him today, and could not keep her face from lighting. "Ole? Come in, come in. It is cold."

He stepped in, his feet shedding snow, and held her with his earnest gaze, so she could not move.

"Is there something I can do for you, Ole?"

"Ja. Perhaps."

"Would you like a warm drink? I have some broth on the hob."

He shook his head and, with the door shut behind him, hauled off his hat. His hair tumbled over his forehead, and helpless reaction seized Lissi in the gut.

Ach, she loved this man.

"Lissi," he said, and the word was a caress. "Lissi, forgive me."

Heat rushed over her. "For what?"

"All your generosity. All the good you have done for us, for me and Hanne—for all the village. Yet I neglected to make sure you had a wish."

"I do not need one." She lied, she lied! She wished for his love, above all things.

"I hope you will accept this one, all the same." He pulled off his mitten and, from within it, produced something which he extended between his fingers. Small and fragile, it trembled slightly as he presented it to her with the slightest of bows.

Lissi blinked in astonishment. Looking impossibly tiny trapped in Ole's big hand, a single, delicate snowdrop lifted its head.

"Ole!" Her wondering gaze flew from the flower to his face. "Is it real?"

"It is."

"Where did you find it?"

"Blooming in the snow. Making its way up from beneath the cold. From beneath the darkness, Lissi, and the despair. Take it, please. Take it from me, and with it the wish you deserve."

Like a woman in a dream, Lissi reached out and plucked the flower from his fingers. So tender was it she expected it to droop, but nay, it continued lifting its head.

"Make your wish, Lissi. Close your eyes and make your wish."

Lissi closed her eyes. She could hear the crackling of the fire behind her, and the wind outside. She could hear Ole—warm and safe and strong—breathing.

For what to wish? She could imagine only one thing, but she did not want to be selfish, given this precious miracle.

She wanted to be happy again. But even more, just like Hanne, she wanted Ole to be happy.

She wished, and wished hard, as such a miracle deserved.

"Lissi."

She opened her eyes when Ole took her in his arms. She could smell the cold on him, and the wool of Papa's coat, and the particular smell, of woodsmoke and male, that meant Ole.

When he kissed her, she closed her eyes again. She saw beautiful things—sunlight and a white dress covered with embroidery, and the three of them cozy beside a fire.

She saw a new babe, in her arms.

Ach, the magical things wishes could accomplish, when shared!

The kiss lasted a long time, and warmed Lissi clear through. When at last it ended, Ole laughed unsteadily and said, "It seems you wished for a kiss."

"For many of them. A supply unending. And bright days. Warm nights, and much laughter. And—and singing."

"To be happy again?"

"To be happy again."

"Lissi, will you marry me?"

271

She backed up, just enough to look into his eyes. "Ole Andersen! Are you sure that is what you want?"

"Sure, ja. I have learned something about love. It is bottomless, like—like a well that never runs dry. The more you give of it, the more there is. And it springs up, just like that flower in your hand."

"Wrong, then, to try and keep it pent up in the heart."

"A terrible sin."

"Maybe that's the true magic."

"Nay, you are the magic." And he kissed her again. A well of love, unending.

Epilog

No one suggested the wedding should wait for spring, even though a wedding in the depth of winter couldn't be celebrated the same way as one in balmy weather, with flowers and sunshine.

Ole said he didn't want to wait, and even though a dusting of new snow fell the night before Lissi's wedding day, she did not mind.

She had the dress, the one Thora had given her, and Mitte said Reverend Pedersen had decorated the church, though Lissi found that difficult to believe. Such a gloomy man, the good reverend. At least he had been, before Mitte got her hands on him.

"Do I look all right?" she asked Mitte now, turning to face her old nurse before leaving for the church.

"You are beautiful, so beautiful." Mitte wept openly.

"Hanne?" Of course her soon-to-be daughter was there, helping Lissi prepare. Lissi had cut down the yellow gown for her to wear, and she looked bright as a jonquil.

Hanne's eyes were round. "You are beautiful!"

"You approve, then?" Lissi did not ask merely about the dress.

Hanne nodded. "I can barely remember Papa so happy."

"Is he nervous?" Mitte asked with a kindly smile.

"I do not think so. Merely—merely excited for the wedding."

"The whole village is excited." Mitte's smile turned to a grin. "We have needed something to celebrate, all of us."

Lissi dimpled. "I am happy to please. Though the weather does not look promising."

"It would not dare snow on my girl's head."

Nay, even a storm would hesitate to displease Mitte.

"Are we ready to go?"

"I think so." Hanne had made Lissi a bouquet of paper flowers, since there were no real ones. That made Lissi remember. "Ach, wait."

The tiny snowdrop had since shriveled to a mere delicate fragment. But she'd wrapped it in a bit of blue cloth and now tucked it into her bosom, next to her heart. "Ready."

The church was draped all in white and green, great swaths of ribbon over the altar and the ends of the pews. All the village appeared to be there ahead of them. Everyone stood in the porch and beamed with smiles, Arne and Solveig standing together. They would be the next to wed. Old Master Shou, and Ebba, and those others who had scarcely been out of their beds since before the sickness arrived.

Inside, Ole waited beside the altar with Reverend Pedersen, who had a green plume pinned to his coat.

Ole wore Papa's coat, and he stood tall, like the proudest man in the village. The proudest man in all the world.

His gaze embraced Lissi when she came in. It cradled her all the way down the aisle. When she reached him, he took her hand in his, firm and warm. Of all the things she later recalled from her marriage, she remembered that best.

Words were spoken. When Ole kissed her, a chaste kind of kiss—for, after all, they were in church—everyone cheered.

Even Reverend Pedersen smiled.

As they went back down the aisle, joined in hand and heart, the survivors of Gjerhold fell in behind him. Someone—Lissi thought it was Holger, from the deep baritone—began singing, and they all joined in. No hymn, this, but a far older song of joy and celebration.

A song of love, triumphant.

And beneath the cold blanket that covered the ground, a thousand snowdrops prepared to bloom.

www.ingramcontent.com/pod-product-compliance
Lightning Source LLC
Chambersburg PA
CBHW051533260626
47170CB00003B/911